asrevniinversa

Solomon Oliver Black

Grosvenor House
Publishing Limited

This book is published by
Grosvenor House Publishing Ltd
Link House
140 The Broadway, Tolworth, Surrey, KT6 7HT.
www.grosvenorhousepublishing.co.uk

This book is a work of fiction. Any resemblance to
people or events, past or present, is purely coincidental.

A CIP record for this book
is available from the British Library

ISBN 978-1-83615-022-0
eBook ISBN 978-1-83615-023-7

For my wife, Jacky
For my children, Jordan, Ashleigh and Ben
For my dog, Alfie

The very best that's happened to me.
The very best that is still happening.
And long may it be.
I am so proud of you all. I love you all
And I'm so lucky to be loved by you all

What could go wrong?
You may already know.

THEN

"Hola, soy Alma. Gracias por llamar. Por favor, deja tu nombre, tu número y un breve mensaje, y me pondré en contacto contigo tan pronto como sea posible. Gracias."

"Alma, it's Matthias. I'm looking for Eva... if you're there, please pick up."

1:33

Matthias was sat in the old, charred and ripped leather wingback armchair.

He didn't know why he was sitting here. Nor why he couldn't move properly? It was like he was stuck in treacle.

Behind him, the French doors that lead out to the rear garden were wide open, letting in the dawning sunlight and the fresh spring morning breeze, which occasionally fluttered the varying colours of the Post-it notes scattered all over the old wooden floor. On each note - black ink scribbles of assorted random shapes and thickness.

The smell of the room was a mix of damp and dust and wood and metal, floating over the top of tobacco, sulphur, and a metallic tang. An unpleasant odour, but not unbearable.

To his left, on the chimney breast, the ornate marble fireplace surround framed the aging open fireplace with its old iron grate. On the mantelshelf stands a half empty glass of dirty brown, grey, cloudy water; a degrading cigarette butt resting and peeling at the bottom. It had been there for a while, he figured.

On the chimney breast itself, above the marble mantel of the fireplace surround, was a rectangle shape, outlined by lighter shades of peeling and cracked plaster and peeling wallpaper. Something had been there, at the centre point of the room. At the bottom right of the rectangle patch a waning handprint, left behind like a spectral reminder of whoever's hand it had been.

At the foot of the fireplace, on the hearth and trickling onto the living room floor, the remnants of what had made the faded shape on the wall - a broken Regency mirror; its frame snapped and its glass in splinters and shards amongst the rainbow mosaic of paper notes.

Matthias's cracked reflection looked back at him. *I look grey and haggard. My unruly beard. I need a shower and a shave… like I've aged… How will she recognise me? Where did that thought come from? Of course she would.* He was overthinking again, trying to control things. He couldn't, he knew. It wasn't important. What was important was for him to hold his nerve, gather what courage he could to give him strength.

Almost directly ahead of him was the old sofa. It needed reupholstering to hide the stains and faded fabric. At one end of the sofa - the end nearest the living room doorway in the right-hand corner of the room from his seated point of view - atop the worn cushion seats, a purple blanket was scruffed up into a bundle and nestled into the corner against the broken armrest. The blanket looked soft and inviting and seemed to exude a gentle warmth in the room's chill.

A smartphone, its screen cracked, lay on the floor at the foot of the sofa.

Glancing to his right, over the floor's wash of coloured notes and ink, Matthias saw the dried blackish streak marks along the skirting board leading to the living room doorway. Following the streaks from where he was sat, he could see the farmhouse's front door and its entrance into the hallway foyer.

It all felt familiar, somehow. Though none of it was making sense in his head.

He lowered his head and looked again at the colours on the floor, which were steadily dissipating beneath the slowly elongating shadow caused by the dawn rising behind the leather armchair.

The click... creak... clack of the front door opening and closing made him look up, and he stared out through the living room doorway. There, in the foyer, stood a woman. She wore a black three-piece suit. Her long black hair hung down straight over her horseshoe waistcoat and brushed the patterned purpure silk pocket square's point, which peered out from her jacket's breast pocket. Her bare feet confirmed to him who she was. Dressed almost exactly as she was when she had told him to come back here.

Alma.

The room's odour changed. It got worse. Not quite a stench, but more of a stink.

Matthias stared at Alma with tunnel vision, everything in his peripheral now obscured.

Alma stepped into the open doorway but didn't enter the living room. "It took me for some time to find you, Matthias. Is long time." Alma spoke in her gravelly, nasally, Spanish-tinged broken English.

Her voice triggered snippets of memories. "What?" he asked, puzzled. "You already found me, Alma. At the... at..." he can taste coffee. "You... you promised me Eva wanted to speak to me -"

"I do, Matt."

Her voice rattled him and made his stomach flip and his heart skip.

His peripheral vision returning, Matthias saw Eva sitting at the end of the sofa, the purple blanket cradled up against her midriff and up across her chest. She looked the same, but different. It was Eva. He could see that. He could sense it was her face, wearing her reading glasses, but her once glowing

4

hair now looked limp and lank. She was as beautiful as he had ever seen her.

Matthias smiled at seeing her again. "Eva? Eva... I've missed... I miss you... so much... it's... you... how are you? You... you were... you're...", he asked, he talked, but he was unable to form a comprehensible sentence. The words getting jumbled and lost in the pictures in his mind, which were blurry and unfocused.

"I'm okay, Matt," Eva smiles back. "Alma is taking care of me."

Over Eva's left shoulder, he looked to Alma, who, still framed by the doorway, had her right arm bent across her body, hand over her heart, near her silk pocket square.

Alma says, "I take Eva to my hea -"

Matthias gave Alma a glare, "Sh!" he scowled. Not just because he didn't want to hear what she had to say, he didn't want to hear her voice. It put his teeth on edge. He wanted some quiet to help him think. Help him make sense of what was in his head.

But the hush in the room wasn't helping at all. He felt acutely aware that he was losing Eva. Losing her to Alma. He stared hard at Alma's dark eyes.

Then, as if she had read his thoughts, Alma stepped into the room, then up to Eva, and placed her right hand on Eva's left shoulder. It seemed a very deliberate move.

Matthias looked back at Eva, but the words he wanted to say were still lost in the mix, and stuck beneath the lump in his throat.

Eva watched him in silence. She could see clearly that Matt was grappling with his own mind, his memories and visions. She so wanted to give him more time, though she knew Alma would struggle with it.

"Why did you call me, Matt?" Eva asked. Not just to break the silence but deciding to give Matt something specific to think about, to focus on. Besides, she'd asked to speak to him, so keeping the conversation moving seemed the right thing to do.

Why did I call you? Matthias looked down at the cracked smartphone on the floor, expecting its screen to light up. It doesn't. The device stays totally black. He thought he recalled a feeling of unease, "I... I was worried," he replied, although it sounds like a question.

Alma bent down and kissed Eva's cheek, then looked over at Matt. "You should have the patience, Matthias. Gary Barlow cantó de paciencia. Gary Barlow -"

"Shut up, Alma. Please -" Matt barked.

"Don't, Matt, she's right. You should've been patient," said Eva, reaching up to hold Alma's resting hand. "The phone distracted me. You called me and I forgot where I was, what I was supposed to be doing."

Another moment popped into his head, "He said no phones -"

"He said no guns, too." Eva responded quickly, with an air of indifference. "Ironic, eh?"

"Is Alanis Morissette," Alma piped up.

Matthias's mind filled with images and thoughts he didn't want, didn't comprehend. "I know. I know. But I warned them. I said..." Maybe they were just dark, twisted visions, daydreams. Or were they memories? Maybe it wasn't real. The lump in his throat ached and felt it was getting heavier. "The gun's gone now. It's... it's in the... garden... you're... I never wanted it... this. I didn't plan for it, Eva," he could feel his own tears burning.

"I know, I know -"

"This has been really hard for me, Eva. Really hard."

"It's not exactly been easy for me, Matt. You could've just given it a half-hour."

"You could've put the phone on vibrate."

"And you could've been patient."

"Is Gary Barlow -"

"Just a bit more self-control, that's all, Matt. That's all you needed."

"It wasn't about control, Eva. It wasn't. I promise it wasn't. You know me. I was anxious, worried. I remember... I hadn't heard from you. I waited. I thought you'd be back, be... be here. I didn't know what else to do. I didn't... I know it's my fault." he choked back a sob.

Eva knew what he was going through, where he was at in his own head, "I didn't ask Alma to set this meeting up to argue with you or blame you, Matt," she tried to reassure him, but she knew he needed a push to help him understand. "None of this is your fault. You'll learn that. I... I just wanted to see you... to... to tell you I love you. I didn't say it enough... don't say it enough. But I did... I do."

Hearing Eva tell him this, Matt felt his heart flutter, butterflies jiggle in his belly. He felt the tears burn his eyes. He felt happiness. No, not the right word. Joy. Joy and peace. Yes, that was it. He felt joy and peace seeping into his body. He tried to get up from the chair, but it was like he was stuck to the leather. With a furrowed brow of confusion, he caught Eva's eyes again.

"We need to get accustomed to this... this different... different way. I need Alma." Eva explained.

"Me estoy cansando, Eva. Necesitamos avanzar," Alma says to Eva.

Eva nods an acknowledgement to Alma without taking her eyes off Matthias. "We need to go. Alma's getting tired." She glances at Alma and responds to her, "Dame un momento más, por favor."

"So, it's all Alma now, eh?" Matt said, surprising himself how calmly and quietly he had said it.

"You do know why it's Alma, Matt," she tried to nudge him along, get him on the same page.

Matthias was a little taken aback by Eva's statement. He'd hoped Eva's words would mean she'd choose him. He took a beat or two, then responded, still calmly at first, "No, I don't know. Why is it Alma, Eva? You were on the sofa. I held you. I comforted you with your blanket, that purple blanket." His agitation was building, clear in his voice's rising volume. Images flooded his mind's eye. "Where did... why did you? I don't want this, Eva. I can't just let you go. I can't let Alma have you. I didn't choose this. I don't choose this."

"Todavía estás aguantando, Matthias. Esta perdido. Desaparecido. Es nuevo ahora," Alma said to Matthias. "Bono, he say –"

"What!? What are you on about? Gary fuckin' Barlow? Bono? I thought you were tired!?", Matthias exploded his venom at Alma.

Alma was not fazed by his outburst. She simply leant forward, took Eva's left hand in her own left hand. Her long fingers, tipped with long, bright white nails, wrapped around Eva's. She whispered in Eva's ear.

Matt gave Alma a black look, then stared coldly at the tableau in front of him. He didn't like the way she was the one holding Eva's hand. He didn't like the black tattooed stripes on her long, spindly fingers. Four on the index finger - two on each of the top larger phalanges, before the untainted end of her finger reached her long, painted nails. The same was repeated on the middle finger, *Two, four... six, eight...* The ring finger, *ni...* Actually, there's a blacker, fresher stripes on her ring finger's proximal phalange. *Two, four... six, eight... te -*

Eva realised that Matt needed to work it all out and accept fate in his own time, as hard as that would be. For now, she knew she needed to deal with the other reason he was here. "Alma needs the key, Matt. Your pocket," she nods at him.

Her voice brought him out of his thoughts and gave the comfort it always did. Matthias reached into his pockets and pulled out his sooty silver cigarette case, a rusting, blackened mortice key, and some charred lolly sticks. He held out his open hands.

Eva laughed, "Oh, the lolly sticks. I always loved that game. Loved our time there, Matt. Beautiful place," she said, and smiled happily at Matt. "Alma doesn't need those," she chuckled. "Just the key. Just drop the key on the floor. Your case...you got any smokes left?" she asked.

Disturbing the layer of soot, smudge marks appearing, Matthias opened the cigarette case and displayed the solitary cigarette within. Eva raises her eyebrows in question to Alma and smiled softly. Alma, after a short pause, gave a subtle nod, and stepped forward to give Matt the Zippo.

"What? We need permission from Alma now?" Matt asked with a touch of cynicism but allowed Alma to drop the silver Zippo into his open right hand.

Eva simply smiled, "Just enjoy, Matt," she said, nodding at him.

He smiled. Then enjoyed the sound and functionality of his Zippo as he sparked up his final smoke. He inhaled deeply, felt the smoke travel down through his chest. Christ, he needed it.

"I asked to see you, Matt, to speak to you because... you need to understand. I know they'll be a million things flying around your head. Things you don't want to be in there. You need to let go now. Let it end."

"I can't let it end like this. I can't let Alma have you. I don't want this."

"You've no choice, Matt. It won't be like this forever. Not forever, I promise. Just give this… this time… give it closure," Eva stated, as she furled up the purple blanket in her lap.

"Cierre." Alma nodded, picked up the key, then turned and walked out into the hallway and toward the farmhouse front door.

That word? Matt felt bile rising from his gut to his throat. He swallowed. Hard.

The click and creak of the front door opening.

Eva pulled the purple blanket close to her and squeezed it. She smiled, "I can go see my mother now, Matt. I'm okay. I love you… always." she says.

"I love you so much, Eva… Wh… A -" he remembered.

"And?" asked Eva, knowing where Matt's mind was going.

"Yes… and And."

"Yes, And."

Clack. The front door closes.

* * * * *

The thick stink in the room faded back to an unpleasant odour, and the coloured Post-it notes fluttered in the breeze and bore witness to the morning spring sunshine as it lengthened and stretched the shadow of the old leather armchair until it reached the empty sofa.

I | A

i speak with her   forked road anxiety
      path to walk   take the path
summer for sale   dancing naked
penis   the stone sparkles toys cluttered
       the woman with the beautiful face
kitchen worktop   matt is there
     shades of purple woman shouts man shouts
          nurturing nurturing nurturing
       embarazada   three cigarettes
      mauve and violet door slams
                      autumn

         the cupboard wrong cupboard

        i am liminal
   silver silver silver glints and sparkles   heartbeat
heartbeat heartbeat hearbeat crossroads

   the lakes   on his knee
         the bridge
grabbing the toys i love you   two
        no lies no secrets yellow
car
birdsong just because
      matt is rambunctious

tell me talk to me guide

four

nina nonata

he loves me

six

i know the woman is not coming
home   destiny fate
the land is   green and fair

diamond

ring

child heartbeat **heartbeat** heartbeat

joy

television ten thousand stations switch in on mesmerise
the girl   egomaniacal egomaniacal **egomaniacal**
     mirror   lolly sticks   no words
spoken in the home   nina nonato

money

i saw you there

matthias writing creating for she
     black car   the big house
   chimney smoke
only when you feel so low do your feelings show

eight

colours   ink ink   i need to hear you

speak

like water   fingers

2:32

The evening light was fading, and the late winter's chill was in the air as she approached the old farmhouse from the frosted lane, passing the SOLD sign. Her duffle bag held what she thought she'd need.

She didn't like to come to this place, the house, too often. She hated it. And she particularly hated it in the winter. The memories...

But needs must.

The whole house was bathed in an eerie blue and grey from the twilight coming in through the dirty windows. Her first task would be to light a candle or two or three in each room. She needed to see while she worked. And they'd need to be scented ones, to make in-roads into vanquishing the odour in the house.

The living room exuded an unsettling stillness as she stepped through the doorway. The air hung heavy with an expected melancholy, and the flickering candlelight struggled to pierce the shadows that clung to the corners of the room. On the floor, scattered and fluttering like spectral confetti, were Post-it notes of various colours. Some clung to the walls, while others twirled through the air, carried by an otherworldly breeze seeping in from the French doors that led into the overgrown garden. Each note bore cryptic scribbles and lines, their significance lost in the murkiness of time.

Her gaze was first drawn to the marble mantelpiece, where, perched close to the edge of the right-hand side of its shelf, stood an undisturbed glass of stale water, a cigarette butt slowly disintegrating at the bottom, giving it a dirty brown-grey tinge. A leftover from the recent past.

Above the mantelpiece, a rectangle shape on the chimney breast where the mirror had once been, clearly placed to be the room's focal point. The shape darker than the surrounding walls; sunlight unable to fade the wall's colour like it had done to the surrounding plaster and old wallpaper. The Regency's gilt frame and its mirrored glass lay broken on the hearth at the foot of the fireplace. Her face's reflection in the splinters and fragments of the shattered glass was a tableau of flickering light and dark amidst the candlelight. Her dark eyes focused on the handprint stain down to the bottom right of the rectangle. Another remnant echoing the past.

She hovered her own hand over the stain, closed her eyes. She knew it would not be easy to clean.

To her right, an old sofa - its fabric worn and faded, which made its dried stains more prominent - stood a foot or so from the hallway partition wall. Opposite it, in the front of the open French doors, the back of the leather wingback armchair presented itself, its seat facing outward through the French doors to the garden. She stepped round to the other side of the chair and saw the charred figure of a man. A haunting silhouette against the dancing candlelight shadows. His form bore the scars of an unforgiving fire, rendering him a spectral embodiment of destruction.

The ashen remnants of clothing and melted leather clung to the figure, their fabrics twisted and blackened by the merciless flames that had consumed them. The skeletal remains of outstretched limbs, the charred flesh frozen in a macabre dance of agony. The air hung heavy with the acrid scent of scorched leather and wood, and smouldered remnants and burnt flesh, a lingering testament to the fire that had claimed the figure.

The facial features, distorted by the heat of the inferno, etched with an eerie expression - a frozen mask of pain and anguish that told a silent tale of the fiery ordeal. Hollow eye sockets stared into the void, devoid of life but brimming with the haunting echoes of the final moments.

The charred figure seemed to exist in a state of perpetual twilight, caught between the realms of the living and the spectral. As it loomed in the shadows, an unsettling presence clung to its form, a testament to the indelible mark left by the flames that had consumed both flesh and soul.

In the stillness of the forgotten space, the burned figure cast an unsettling pallor—a ghostly reminder of a tragic fate that had left its mark on the ephemeral fabric of existence. The remnants of the man, forever frozen in the inferno's aftermath, whispered of a story unfinished, a tale of fiery transformation that lingered in the eerie, charred contours of his spectral form.

How the pain of fire could be more welcome than the pain of grief, she didn't know. It wasn't her place to know. Or understand.

At the corpse's foot lay a Zippo, its silver blackened by the fire.

This horrific sight was now the focal point of the room.

* * * * *

After a while, she decided she'd done all she could - all she had the energy for. She could do no more at this point. She knew what she needed to do next, and she'd need her strength and her patience for the task.

It'll take effort

It'll take some time.

3:31

In the fading late afternoon light, the air carried the crisp bite of deepening winter.

He stood amidst the clump of evergreen bushes, shovel in hand.

The shovel had been easy to find in the garage, resting against a cobwebbed wall amongst old tools and tins and nails and screws - a few of the things left behind by previous owners, he'd assumed. The patch of earth crunched beneath his boots as he surveyed the chosen spot. In the twilight, the trees cast long shadows, creating an eerie tableau that seemed to whisper the secrets he didn't want to hear.

He cut a sombre figure as he dug with a steady rhythm. The sound of the shovel striking the earth punctuated the hushed stillness. The soil, chilled by the encroaching cold, resisted each turn of the blade, as if reluctant to yield to the inevitability of its purpose. His breath hung in the air, a visible testament to the chill that settled into the marrow of his bones.

The winter sky, painted in hues of fast-fading amber and darkening blues and greys, framed a murmuration of starlings. Their survival dance casting a solemn and sardonic backdrop against this solitary act, watching silently as he worked. In the quiet solitude of his task, as the hole deepened with the echo of each shovel scoop, memories surfaced, carrying the weight of where this story had reached. He pondered the shattering of destiny, of the cycle of life and death, reflecting on the transient nature of existence. *Samsara.* He'd used that in a recent story he'd written. *Not the time for irony,* he thought.

The hole was as deep as he was going to make it.

The early evening moon, obscured by wisps of ominous clouds, cast an ethereal glow as he emerged from the shadowy confines of the house, his burden cradled within the folds of the purple blanket. The creaking floorboards had groaned in sympathy with the weight of the task at hand, and the wind whispered through the trees and bushes outside, carrying with it an unsettling chorus.

His silhouette, elongated by the moonlight, moved with a measured solemnity, navigating the path from house to grave with an eerie grace. The purple-wrapped form in his arms seemed to possess a spectral weight, as if the essence of the departed soul clung to the fabric. The rhythmic crunch of leaves beneath his boots echoed through the night, punctuating the silence with an unsettling cadence.

As he approached the open grave, the air thickened with an intangible tension. The grave, now a void in the moonlit ground, awaited its silent occupant. He removed the blanket. He wanted to take a last long look at the face, though he didn't want to remember her like this. Even if it was for such a short time. He lowered her body into the waiting earth as gently as he could, with a reverence and benediction the moment deserved. The haunting glow of the moon painted the scene in a diaphanous blue pallor and cast a disquiet upon the ceremony unfolding beneath its watchful gaze.

In this choreography between life and death, he felt the weight of the departed soul settle into the cold embrace of the earth. The blanket, now a symbol of transition, fluttered momentarily in the breeze, whispering secrets only the grave knew. As he backfilled the soil, the onset of night seemed to draw a veil over the unwanted ceremony, leaving only the echoes of rustling leaves and the enigmatic stillness of the do-it-yourself cemetery in its wake.

Slamming the shovel upright into the earth and draping the purple blanket over the handle, he felt alone, yet strangely a step closer to her and to closure.

Retracing his steps back to the house, a heavy silence hung in the air, broken only by the rustle of the trees and bushes in the breeze. The memories of the solemn task he had just completed clung to him like an intangible weight, intensifying the shadows that enveloped the unfamiliar surroundings of this old farmhouse they'd planned to make their home.

He suddenly felt the weight of what he'd done. Not guilt. Pain. Pain inside his chest, in his stomach. Then, in his pocket, he felt the bump of the key. What was he supposed to do with the key? It was no use to him now.

Stepping through the French doors, the echoes of the creaking floorboards in the living room seemed to reverberate with the solemnity of the story that had unfolded thus far. She was now in her final resting place, but she'd left an indelible mark on the atmosphere within.

Distraught and burdened by the weight of grief, he stood in the dimly lit space, his breath hitching as he grappled with the emotions swirling within him. The late evening breeze coming in through the open doors fluttered and lifted the multi-coloured Post-it notes that littered the floor; pinks and greens and yellows and blues and oranges and purples swirled around his ankles and knees. Remembering when they'd been stuck on the wall - the message thereon - then their violent flight around the room, stripping them from the living room wall and dropping them on the floor, he felt the walls closing in on him, amplifying the ache of loss.

The echoes of life now ended reverberated through the empty rooms, creating an unsettling symphony of quiet sorrow. The moon cast a pale glow through the windows, bearing witness to the aftermath of an unfathomable series of events. Enveloped in the darkness of his despair, he was now faced with the reality that the walls of the house, and out into the garden, had all become a mausoleum of bad memories.

Exhausted from the grief and labour, he sank slowly and deliberately into the torn leather wingback armchair. He'd turned the chair around to face out to the garden, partly visible through the French doors. He'd turned the chair, so it no longer faced the sofa. He didn't want to face the sofa.

Another unwanted memory filled his mind with images he didn't want to see. He didn't want to remember any of it anymore. He didn't want to remember her like this. Buried. He didn't want to remember. Not a moment more of the loss. He'd endured it for long enough. He'd held on to the hope of talking to her again... But that had been too painful. He recalled he'd heard a song that sang something about already losing something despite holding it tightly. *Bono*, he thought. He wished he could remember that.

* * * * *

The petrol was cold as it hit his head, forcing his mop of hair down over his brow, his eyes tightly closed. His lips and teeth rattled together as he tried to keep from getting the liquid in his mouth. He felt the petrol seep into his beard, drip down his chin, soak the collar of his shirt, cascade down the front of the material and leaching through inside and underneath, cold and wet against his chest. Now it was being absorbed through his jeans.

The silver engraved Zippo lighter was a beautiful item. It was a treasured gift she'd given him. She'd called it tacky, but he loved it. Loved its design, its simplicity, its reliability. The recognisable sound it made - the opening clink, the rasp of the flint, the closing clunk.

As numb as he felt, he knew he'd feel pain for a few moments.

He heard the clink.

He heard the rasp of the flint.

He dropped the lighter into his lap...

He didn't hear the clunk.

4:30

Not really comprehending where the feeling or the need came from, but with a sense of urgency gnawing at his core, Matthias rushed back to the living room, his footsteps echoing in the space like a frantic heartbeat.

As soon as he entered, the sight on the sofa jolted him back to the reality of it all. Above his head, through the ceiling and bleeding in through the open living room door, he could, once again, hear the old plumbing flushing and whooshing and clanging and gurgling and pinging and tinging and tanging. Then something scraped and thudded down each step on the staircase. Glass cracked and crashed. He spun his head to listen, to try to pick up where the sounds were coming from; to look, to get a visual on the auditory. The glass of water on the mantel trembled, shaking the cigarette butt within. Crashing and splintering sounds crept in from dining room. The floorboards in the hallway creaked. A squeak traversed right to left along the streaked skirting board in front of him. The kitchen chairs sent through their high-pitched squeal before the clattering onto the linoleum. An acrid, putrid smell of tobacco and sulphur and gunpowder and rotten eggs and dust drove up into his nostrils.

Matt stood still and stared at the wall of the semi-assembled Post-it notes. He then stared down at the rest of the notes and pads on the floor. He wasn't afraid. Right then he felt no fear, just the need to scrawl the black marker pen on every one of the coloured notes.

Dropping to his knees, he began scratching and doodling black ink shapes and lines onto the paper. Ink on note, ink on note, ink on note. Again and again and again. Meaningless scribbles that just added to the shape of the chaotic mosaic of a broken, graffitied rainbow feathering the floor around him.

With very few pieces of paper left inkless, he began sticking them on the wall. Slowly at first, then quicker and quicker and quicker and quicker. The montage forming before him meant nothing to him. Revealed nothing. Showed nothing but coloured squares and black ink.

He added more and more to the wall. Quicker still. Faster and faster and faster. Something was taking shape.

As he moved note after note, changing their positions on the wall - one, two, three, more-at-a-time - the colours and lines, the jumble of colours and shapes seemed to dance in front of his eyes, until his vision blurred and he fell backwards and landed horizontally on the floor, staring up at the ceiling.

The eerie orchestra of sounds and noises abated, and the smell receded.

Sitting up, he saw the word laid out clearly on the wallcovering –

'CIERRE'.

He had no fucking idea what that meant.

Still staring at the word before him, he glanced to his left at the sofa and the purple shape thereon. Sadness welled up within him, making him struggle for a decent breath.

The French doors creaked ajar. Then they were sucked open by the evening's breeze. The chill drifted around his feet, up around his ankles, as he stood himself upright. He could feel the air spiralling up and around until it was lifting the Post-its and sending them fluttering all around him in a noisy, flapping frenzy, tearing the notes and the word from the wall, like a colourful scream of swifts; a thousand little paper birds swooping around him, their wings beating. The blur and noise all around him for only a moment or two, before all the colours dropped to the floor.

Then stillness.

Then silence.

Then, what he could only describe as a voice - though he knew it wasn't a voice; not produced by a larynx of any human description. It came from behind him, from the fireplace, the chimney breast, and it guided him to what he'd been looking for all along: a way to bring all this to a close.

Raising his eyes up from the floor of colour, his heartbeat increased as he gazed once more at the sofa. He knew what he had to do. But he didn't have the energy to do it. Not right now. Not yet.

He laid down and closed his eyes.

N | D

path to walk   take the path
summer   matt is there

                                    matt is there
shades of purple woman shouts man shouts
              nurturing nurturing nurturing lies hands
up   embarazada denial   three cigarettes

                                    autumn
the man hitting the man   he lied
              pistol weighed heavy

                        i am liminal
                                        child
heartbeat heartbeat heartbeat hearbeat
pick up the toy colours pictures echoes   use it
              the lakes shouting matt
              backlash
                        i love you   two
heavy toy   lies
    the child standing   silence
                                        money
                        matt   rambunctious
              writing

25

time is not linear its irregular

nina nonata   narcissist man

he loves me

me she to edify   **six**

i know the woman is not coming

home   **destiny fate**

and i feel and

diamond

ring footsteps **footsteps** footsteps

grievous   man in

the glasses holds the child heartbeat heartbeat **heartbeat**

the child

to be talked about

no more   bodily   **joy**

egomaniacal egomaniacal **egomaniacal**

words spoken

harm   venerable man   not

venerable

money

matthias writing creating for she me

only

when you feel so low do your feelings show

they are my dreams i will dream them

negotiate not offer   love is turmoil

eight

colours   ink ink

          like water   fingers fingers

5:29

Matthias made his way to the basement, pretty much in a daze.

He'd moved slowly through the house's darkness. His eyes bulged and his pupils were large, trying to draw in what little light there was. He held his hands out in front, feeling and fumbling his way, when his eyes couldn't adjust quick enough to the blackness.

Arms a little out to his side, he used his palms and fingers against the cold walls to guide himself down the pitch black of the concrete stairs to the basement, treading carefully and slowly until he bumped into the wooden door. He dropped to his knees and stared at it. Well, it was pitch black, so he couldn't see the door, but he felt the wood in front of him, so he knew the door was there.

This was the third time he'd been in the house, and aware that he'd only been in the basement briefly during the previous two visits - probably only a for a minute or so, no more - and wishing he could forget all about it. He'd put the three of them in there, sure. But he'd done it in the dark. He pulled the basement door key out of his pocket and thumbed and rolled it between his fingers. He then put it back and felt it nestle into the lolly sticks.

No way did he want to go in there

"What am I supposed to do with you fuckers?" he asked at the door, smacking it hard with a flat palm.

He rubbed his right hand around and found the door handle, rattled it a bit, the door still locked firmly shut. Then, running his right hand just below the handle, he found the keyhole. He lowered his head, and he sniffed it. The fetor made him pull his head back, sharply. It was rank.

He turned and sat and rested his back against the door, then thumped the back of his head against the door twice in quick succession. "What the fuck is going on, you cunts? Fuckin' tell me!" he pleaded.

Matt had no idea who he was hollering at, or who he expected to reply. He whacked the door again in frustration. And again.

"I wish we'd never set eyes on this house," he muttered to himself. "I should've told you to get fucked... back in the garden. After Eva told me more about her mother, and knowing what a cunt you are, I should've just told you what you could do with your money."

Matt slammed his head twice against the wooden door. "Oh Eva, I should've manned up."

The thought of Eva upstairs at rest gave him no solace from the pain he was feeling. He felt his chest tightening, then trying to catch each stumbling breath as the sobs came. He whacked the door twice more, trying to avert a full flow of tears, sadness and grief.

Matthias found himself staring up the concrete steps to the low evening light trying to break through from the kitchen. "I'm sorry about the gun, babes," he pleaded to Eva. "I'm sorry that this is our destiny, our fate. I love you so much. Loved you so much. I'll always fuckin' love you, Eva. Always."

He sobbed a little more and rubbed the back of his head after slamming it against the door again. "I never liked you, Jude. Never. I loved Eva, and you were her father, but that was it. You were nothing else to me. Nothing! You fuckin' deserved it!"

Tap.

An almost imperceptible single tap from the other side of the door.

"You're in there, aren't you?"

There was no way it could be true, could it?

It made no sense to him. The noise had unnerved Matthias. It made no sense at all. His back to the door, he felt stuck in the dark, his back glued to the basement door. The weak light at the top of the concrete stairs was beckoning, looking more enticing than it had. The urge to be upstairs, back with her, was staggering. He knew he needed to ascend from the darkness.

He needed to act.

6:28

The rattle of the door handle followed by the two thumps against the door made Jude jolt.

Devoid of light, the blackness of the basement, its cold, damp concrete, the boxes and chairs all around, made it claustrophobic. He felt hemmed in. Confined.

He'd put his broken glasses on to see what he could, but there was nothing but dark grey walls, dark grey floor, some boxes and old chairs, and the old wooden door.

He'd tried to stand and stretch, but at six-foot-five, there was no headspace. He'd tried to take a few crouched steps, but there were obstacles on the floor preventing any movement. He couldn't see what the obstacles were, but he knew they were there.

His two Slavic heavies, Gerasim and Draško, were locked in here with him. He knew that... didn't he? Not really conscious of it, but he remembered it. But when he'd called out for them, there'd been no answer. He'd hollered for them a few times - "Gez and Dizzy," he'd bellowed. He'd never tried to pronounce their given names, and he wasn't going to kowtow to cheap, foreign labour now, even in this predicament. He'd had to listen to the two of them whining and moaning about being in here, and he'd told them their complaints were pointless. Besides, the two of them had spent several days hiding from soldiers in some Balkan shop cellar back in the late nineties - if their stories were to be believed - so what they were moaning about this place for, he didn't know.

He wouldn't admit it to himself, but he wanted to hear their whinging now, wanted to just see them whispering and mumbling and muttering to one another. Just to know they were there. He wanted to talk to them, yet they were ignoring him. Yes, they were angry that he'd lied - though he couldn't recall what he was supposed to have lied about – but that didn't give them the right to ignore him. They were angry at being shut up in here, he understood that. But he was the boss. They knew better than to give him the silent treatment.

He put his broken glasses back on, holding the one working arm to keep them steady and level. He squinted through the broken lenses, focusing beyond the cracks and lines of the glass to the basement door. Perhaps he now needed to take the lead and call out beyond the basement. "I don't know if you can hear me, Matty -"

There was a further smack against the other side of the door.

Jude flinched. He was sure he recalled his two goons speaking to Matty earlier. "You both spoke to him, didn't ya? Spoke to Matty. So, I'm trying it. Seems like the right thing to do, yeah?" Jude said to Gez and Dizzy. They didn't reply. "Gez? Diz? You fuckers still ignoring me, eh?"

Another smack on the other side of the wooden door made him flinch again.

Jude had spoken to Matty, what, three times over the past... few hours... days... a week... fortnight? A horrible nagging feeling suddenly struck him that he didn't know how much time had gone by since he'd been stuck in this place. He'd spoken to him in this house, hadn't he? Yes. When they came to see this house, when he'd staked his claim to this basement to hold his retirement wine collection. When he'd plonked himself in that comfortable old leather wingback. Or was that another time?

He couldn't bring it to mind. There was definitely another time they'd spoken. Yes, that was it, he'd spoken to Matty in the garden, when they'd gone round to Eva's to plan the job. They'd smoked. Him a cigar, Matty a cigarette. He recalled something about Matty saying he was giving them up. The memory led Jude to pull a cigar out of his top pocket, only to find no cigar, the pocket missing, and his jacket torn. He patted himself down further, but then gave up. Seemed like déjà vu.

Jude remembered feeling smug, back there in the garden. The planning had gone well; everyone committed to the job. He remembered money -

"I bought you this fuckin' house, Matty! And this is how you treat me!?" he hollered angrily toward the wooden door.

Jude was livid. Eva and Matty had wanted this house, and he'd offered to help them out from the goodness of his heart. And this was the fucking thanks he got. He knew Matty didn't like him, but he expected better from his own daughter. Christ, he'd brought her up on his own, ever since her fucking mother walked out. And he was the bad guy?

"We were both better off when her mother left. She used to nag and flip out over nothin'. Arguments nearly all the fuckin' time… always blaming me for everything that went wrong. Not a great environment to bring up a kid, Matty. Eva knows that." Jude knew he was spouting fabricated nonsense, but his anger was boiling. "I've given her love and care… education… seen her want for nothin', and this is how she treats me!?" he spat. "What's she got to say about this, Matty? Keeping her old man locked up in here?"

Two more smacks hit the wooden door. Louder this time.

"Maybe you're writing a new story, Matty. Writing new colourful stickers to stick on the wall. Pretty colours like a fuckin' rainbow! Ooh, I love you, Eva," he ridiculed. "Is my Eva feeding you some kind of backstory to fit your narrative? For you to bend reality, Matty? You've turned her against me. She's upstairs. You bring her down here and talk to me, do you hear!?"

No response. Silence. Not even a breath.

"Matty! You fuckin' listening to me!? Bring her down here, NOW!" Jude screamed.

A voice? A whisper? A murmur? Jude wasn't sure. His auditory cortices tried to process the new sound he was hearing.

"Is that her? Is that Eva? Get her to talk to me, Matty -"

Eva's voice seeped into his thoughts, but he was not in control of the transmission, simply the receiver,

the kitchen worktop small the cereal box bowls cutlery toast toys cluttered it matt is there the woman sobbing tears pointing at the toys pushing the other items aside the man comes in woman shouts the man held up his hands in denial shook his head the indignation now pointing at a single toy the screaming the crying the denial the man the steel pistol weighed heavy steal my daily bread child sobbing the man put things in the sink cereal in the cupboard the wrong cupboard picking up the toys the toy steal it use it abuse it leave it for dead the shouting recoil from the backlash of what you said sobbing tears eyes stinging matt is watching writing i start to feel alone minutes pass hour hours pass time is not linear its irregular in space in time what is going on outside of your mind what are you hiding from what are you looking for the land is not green and fair its hard to bear and i feel and i feel torment from deep within razor cuts beneath the skin matthias writing creating for me behind the locked door of the big house only when you feel so low do your feelings show voice in my head tears it apart you see she wants to meet me wants to look me in the eye life love harmony born a million lies...

Over and over and over her voice repeated, conjuring memories that Jude didn't want to recall, images he didn't want to see. He found himself sobbing real tears, not his usual crocodile ones. "Where's my Eva, Matty? Where is she?" he sniffed and choked, almost a whisper.

Two heavy bangs hit the door.

"You never asked me, Matty. Eva never asked me..." he sobbed, still trying to push it away, assign the blame elsewhere.

the man held up his hands in denial shook his head the indignation the steel pistol weighed heavy steal my daily bread child sobbing steal it use it abuse it leave it for dead the shouting recoil from the backlash of what you said sobbing tears eyes stinging matt is watching writing what is going on outside of your mind what are you hiding from what are you looking for and i feel torment from deep within razor cuts beneath the skin matthias writing creating for me behind the locked door only when you feel so low do your feelings show voice in my head tears it apart life love harmony born a million lies...

The more Eva's voice permeated his mind, the harder it was becoming for Jude to battle against it, to bury what he knew he knew. Closer and closer it came to the fore.

denial indignation pistol weighed heavy steal my daily bread child sobbing steal it use it abuse it leave it for dead recoil from the backlash of what you said matt is watching writing what are you hiding from what are you looking for torment from deep within razor cuts beneath the skin matthias writing creating for me behind the locked door life love harmony born a million lies...

Was this him? Matty? Was he here, down in the basement? Jude tried his best to put his narcissistic spin on things, turn it back to being all about him while selling a lie or two. "I always liked you, Matty. I might not have shown it, but I always liked you."

Louder and louder, Eva's voice became, repeating, repeating, repeating –

denial indignation pistol weighed heavy steal my daily bread child sobbing steal it use it abuse it leave it for dead recoil from the backlash of what you said matt is watching writing what are you hiding from what are you looking for torment from deep within razor cuts beneath the skin matthias writing creating for me behind the locked door born a million lies...

- over and over and over again, her voice bounced and bundled and throbbed inside his head.

Not knowing what to do - the words eating away at everything he'd ever felt, ever thought, ever done - Jude threw his glasses against the wall and held his head in his hands, mumbling and begging for the voice to cease. Was he giving the words a voice, or a voice to the words?

It was becoming shallower, quieter and quieter and more distant until it faded out with a final repetition –

born a million lies born a million lies born a million lies born a million lies...

"I know you loved Eva..." *Loved?* Past tense. Jude choked back his mumbling, raised his head, and found himself staring at the peaceful faces of Gez and Dizzy. "I could see Eva loved you, so I was happy to help you -"

Eva's voice suddenly returned and screeched repetitively.

denial indignation pistol weighed heavy recoil from the backlash of what you said matthias writing creating for me behind the locked door life born a million lies...

Gez and Dizzy's faces became gaunt, hollowing out.

"Oh, Eva, what do you want?" Jude now felt he was suffocating, smothered by the broken, haunting faces of his two associates. His throat was rough and dry, like swallowing sand. His guts were burning, churning. The cold realisation rose in Jude's insides. The faces faded further away.

born a million lies born a million lies born a million lies born a million lies...

Eva's voice dissipates little-by-little again, as Jude turned to face the wooden door. He slammed his forehead against it...

He knew.

He knew.

"I'm sorry, Matthias."

7:27

Matthias heard the thud then the crash.

He had paused a moment ago, just for a few seconds, when he'd heard a rattle and clatter, which sounded like it came from the kitchen. But this noise had stopped him in his tracks; stopped him tacking Post-it notes on the wall.

This, he knew, came from the dining room.

Hesitating for a moment, then making his way out of the living room and into the hallway foyer, Matt followed the now struggling light from his torch, shining it over the darkened stains on the floorboards, and through into the dining room.

The heavy mahogany table was flipped on its side.

He went to take a step backwards to exit the room but -

Slam!

- the door loudly shut behind him, making him jolt forward and bump into the upturned table, losing his balance, then stumble to the floor, sitting him straight down on his backside.

Catching his breath, taking a moment to slow his heartbeat, he watched as the dining-room door creaked slowly open, darkness bleeding in caressing the edge of the ever-dimming torchlight.

He stayed sat on the floor for a few minutes, waiting uneasily. Waiting for what, he didn't know. And when 'didn't know' didn't happen, he pulled himself to his feet and stepped to the door, and that was when the clattering and scraping of kitchen chairs on kitchen linoleum screeched through the hallway...

The 'didn't know' was happening.

Despite the dread and fear building in his guts, in his chest, Matt charged through to the kitchen, angrily throwing the chairs out of the way, before barrelling down the concrete steps and crashing against the wooden basement door, stunning himself.

The odour seeping out from beneath the basement door, hanging around the bottom of the steps, acted like smelling salts, jarring and kicking his senses and jolted him to consciousness. Just a few seconds or so had passed when he opened his eyes. He knew they were open, wide open, but it was pitch black. So, eyes open or not, he could see nothing. He'd left the torch upstairs. The wooden basement door was at his back, the wood felt rough on the back of his head. His legs were up in an awkward and perplexing position on the bottom two steps he'd just crashed down.

"What the fuck is going on, you fucks!?" he screamed, banging his head twice against the door. "Fuck!". He untwisted himself and smacked the door three more times, screaming one long outburst as he did.

He waited. Breathed. Listened.

Silence.

Matthias was much slower ascending the concrete steps, hobbling to loosen the slight cramp and ache in his legs and lower back.

Through the kitchen, where he slid the chairs out of his way - removing them from his path, rather than applying any force - he made his way back into the dining room. The beam of the torchlight was really struggling now, so he did the age-old trick of removing the batteries, rolling them between his hands - shake 'em to wake 'em, give them a bit of heat - and exhaling his hot breath onto them as he did. Then putting them back in the casing in swapped positions. The beam was a little brighter. Magic. But not great magic. He knew the torch would die in a matter of minutes.

Back in the living room, he felt the evening chill seeping in through the old French doors and old windows, cold against his now sweat-covered skin. He plonked himself down into the leather armchair and stared at where she lay on the sofa, shining the light over the blanket. Not seeing her, but her shape. The shape of loss.

To his right, he stared at the rainbow of notes tacked randomly to the wall, the inky scribes on them just random scrawls. He felt lost. Confused. Agitated. His right leg fidgeting and bouncing up and down.

Another crash from the dining room and a rattle of chairs on linoleum from the kitchen startled him.

* * * * *

"What? Whatwhatwhatwhatwhat? -" Matthias muttered at the floor and at the walls and at the sofa in the living room, as he put more scribbles and scrawls on more of the multicoloured Post-its. "What am I supposed to write, for fuck's sake!?" His latter exclamation was louder and aimed through the open living room door and out into the hallway, to whomever or whatever might hear him.

From the kitchen, he could still hear the chairs scraping on the lino. He then heard a cupboard door slam and a glass clink and the tap run. He could hear the old mahogany dining room table thumping and bumping against the floorboards.

Scribble and tear and discard. Scribble, tear and discard. Inking note-after-note and flipping them away onto the floor. Then gathering them up and adding them to the notes he'd already stuck on the wall. Coloured squares with scratches and scrawls of black ink almost covered the wall at every point he could stretch and reach.

A breath in his ear. A whisper? He couldn't define it as a voice; it was barely audible. Barely discernible. But it said something to him. He started rearranging the Post-its, joining the ink marks, forming shapes.

Sweating, tired, lower back burning, the shape of something was coming into being, yet the noises from the kitchen and dining room continued. The thickness of the air in the room pushed down on his shoulders, making him ache and shake, but still he continued building his strange collage.

A howl and a shriek pierced the stale, heavy air in the house. Panicked and unnerved, Matthias dropped to the floor, picked up the torch, turned, and threw it at the mirror, where it hit the greasy handprint and cracked the glass. Then the slight webbed cracks grew, its lines extending. Suddenly, the glass shattered, sending shards and jagged pieces clattering down onto the mantelpiece, over the grate, and onto the floor.

His back and head resting against the wall of Post-it notes, Matt breathed raggedly, staring at the tableau before him, watching the dying light of the torch flicker off the broken glass. He was very conscious of his breathing pattern changing as, slowly, the frame of the mirror dropped on one side, the corner of the gilt frame resting on the mantelshelf where it pivoted for a second or two, then clattered to the floor.

The last thing he saw, before the torchlight finally died, was the mirror's frame-shaped stain on the now blank wall. And in exactly the same position as it had been when the mirror was in situ, the handprint materialised on the old plaster.

Now, almost in darkness, just the twilight straining in through the French doors' glass, Matthias realised the house was quiet again.

He turned to face the wall of notes. Stuck a few more on the wall, but still none of it made any sense to him.

A crash made him drop the handful of Post-its he was clutching.

V | E

                             road anxiety

      I never saw   **we never spoke**

                        matt is there not there

purple

        nurturing nurturing

   embarazada   three cigarettes

                   man tell me of the

woman flailing her arms hitting the man autumn **hitting**

the man hitting the man   he lied finger on

the steel

              steal steal steal my daily bread

            i am liminal   all i

see is red

            steal it use it abuse it leave it

for dead   recoil

from the backlash of what you said   house

sanctuary   **two**

      the front door   lies

yellow car

                money

arms hold me
time is not linear its irregular **four**

                       narcissist man

he loves me
he does not love me she to edify me **six**

               woman is not coming
home   **perdida**   the red bus

child stay down on the ground
just watching you bleed   man
in the glasses holds the child **heartbeat** heartbeat heartbeat
the child feels him squeeze her shoulders

               pain

     broken sticks   and stones

                   money

               back seat of
a black car **behind the locked door of the big house**
                 only
when you feel so low do your feelings show
they are my dreams i will dream them
     bleed scream crawl
   phone ringing and pinging **and and**

43

eight

ink   nine

8:26

"What do you think Matty's doing?" Gerasim asks Jude.

Jude pulled a cigar from his ripped top pocket and pats himself down in search of a lighter. He hasn't got one. Keeping the cigar in his mouth, he pushed his broken glasses up the bridge of his nose, giving the situation some thought. *Something feels off.*

"He gave it the big threatening words back at the house, didn't he? Over-the-top. All fuckin' mouth, you ask me. He got it wrong." Jude, his brow furrowed in thought, removed his broken glasses and tossed his cigar across the room.

"He can't keep us locked in here, boss, can he?" Gerasim threw the question out rhetorically. "Matty! Matty!" he shouts up at the concrete ceiling above him.

"Shout all you want, Gez. He's not listening."

"You say that, but he heard Draško, didn't he?" Gerasim looked around for his friend but can't see him in the basement's darkness. He kind of recalls that he'd been close to wanting to throw Dras out of the basement. Had he done that? He throws his arms open wide. "Matty can't keep us locked up in here. It's damp, dingy, cold... It fuckin' stinks. He can't. He just can't. It was an accident. He can't blame -"

"Stop fuckin' moaning. You told me you and Dizzy hid out in a cellar in a fuckin' war zone. This ain't a war zone, Gez. It's us down here whilst Matty potters around upstairs doing whatever the fuck he's doing. This is a mistake, that's all. He'll soon realise -"

"But we had -"

Jude stops Gerasim mid-sentence. "You got somethin' else to say?"

Gerasim slides a little further down in his supine position, just his head against the cold concrete wall. The rest of his body lies flat against the cold, damp floor. He knows there's nothing good to be gained by challenging his boss, pointing out his faults. "How come you're so sure of yourself, Jude?"

"I've done nothing wrong. Matty will realise that soon enough."

"Well, he obviously thinks we have. We're locked in here. Matty's locked us in this concrete fuckin' box and... and... he's a cunt! Matty's a cunt. You see what he's done here!? You can fuckin' see it! And you're sitting here with... with nothing -"

"I've always looked out for the pair of you, haven't I?" exclaimed Jude. "Where do you think you'd be now, if I hadn't taken you on, given you work... just left you two to work this country out, survive on your own, hm? Sent back home on a fucking dingy? A prison cell? A fuckin' prison cell, G. With Diz shittin' his fuckin' pants -"

"We might as well be in prison, fuckin' locked in here, Jude. And I'd rather Draško was here shittin' himself."

Gerasim thought about the shop cellar back in Mostar. Gunfire and shouting outside, and Dras complaining about his guts, dropping a couple of smelly shits as he cowered in the darkest corner available. He remembers his sister, Milena, and her friend, Draško's cousin Danika, giggling at Dras's unfortunate condition. It was the girls' fault that the four of them found themselves hiding in the cellar. They'd laughed and ridiculed his friend's predicament. Fucking bitches. And, here now, locked in a basement because of a bitch girl -

Knock-knock from the other side of the door stopped Gerasim mid-thought.

"Matty! Matty! Let us outta here! You absolute cu... Don't blame me -"

A loud crash vibrates through the walls and the door.

The whispers seep into Gerasim's head, a haunting mix of familiarity, *Gerasim. Gerasim. Gez. Gezzz. Gerasiiim* growing into an elongated piercing shriek *GEZZZZ!*

A clatter and a crash from above penetrated the ceiling and came rumbling down the basement steps and through the old wooden door.

"Dras, mate. You here? You heard him. You spoke to him. What did he say, Draško? Dras -"

Gezzz! Gezzz Gezzz

Gerasim gets to his feet. He glares at Jude with judgment and hatred, but mainly with fear distorting his own facial features. He lurches to the door and slaps his palm heavily against it. Again and again and again.

"I'm sorry, I'm sorry. Draško... Draško... Dras... I'm sorry, my friend. Matthias. I'm fuckin' sorry," he sobs. "I... I understand..."

Silence.

Darkness.

9:25

Draško, the whisper says.

To Draško, the hushed, breathy voice emanated from every wall, every corner. "Did you hear that?" he asked, his voice quivering.

Jude and Gerasim shook their heads. They'd heard nothing. Draško had been muttering and rambling, moaning and whining, agitated for - how long? Neither of them knew.

"It wasn't my fault what happened. You bumped into me, Jude, you had... it was not me, Matty knows that... right!? I was just in the wrong place at the wrong time. Things ju-just happen. Sometimes they just happen..." Draško was mumbling again.

Draško. That wretched whisper again. It stretches the vowels, *Draaaškoooooo.* The cry was a nauseating jumble of the past and the present, of male and female.

He stared wide-eyed, eyebrows raised, nostrils flared. "They just happen... I didn't mean it to happen, Ger. She wasn't supposed to follow her out. She wasn't!"

"What is Diz on about? Eva didn't follow anyone out, she was -" Jude stated.

"Eva!? I'm not talking about Eva!" Draško shot back at his boss. "Milena... I'm talking about Milena. Ger knows. She wasn't supposed to follow Danika... she wasn't..."

Gerasim knew what his friend was talking about.

Dras had been embarrassed and angry at his cousin laughing at his bowel affliction, furious enough to throw her out of the cellar. Milena had screamed at him, begged him to reconsider. How could he send his cousin out there, into the hands of soldiers, rapists, murderers? It wasn't right. Dras had shouted that women were ten-a-penny, десет пенија. She could just одјеби и умри and that very likely is what happened. Gerasim had watched Milena's outburst and, quite frankly, Dras had a point. Besides, it was their fault that he and Dras were in this cellar. Gersim was not going to stop his sister following her friend out of the cellar.

The four of them had run when soldiers came through their town. The boys had wanted to fight, wanted to use their young teenage bravado to defend their home, their family. But their parents and grandparents had told them to take the girls and protect them. So, they'd run. He and Dras had not seen their families again. And the best the girls could do was move slowly, shriek a lot, and then drag them into the shop cellar at the first sight of a soldier and the sound of gunfire, and there they were trapped. Just like they were now -

"I would have let her stay, Gerasim, she was your sister. I should not have…"

Gerasim was concerned at seeing how disoriented and disturbed his friend was. The two of them had never spoken of the time back home. He didn't need to. And he believed that Dras shouldn't need to, either. The two of them were burly, strong.

"Should not have what, Dras?" he asked

"Sent Danika out. Let you send Milena out with her. We sent the girls out… we… the soldiers… This is that witch upstairs' fault. It is karma, Ger. Karma. She knew we'd get a gun… we wanted to kill -"

"Dras! They are ten-a-penny, Dras. Girls do not care about you. You were right back then. You are right now. We will get out of here, like we got out of that cellar. You and me, the two of us. We will survive this, Dras. We will," Gerasim cut into Draško's ramblings before he said too much. A glance toward Jude evidenced that he wasn't listening to Dras. Thankfully.

Draaaškoooooo Draaaškoooooo

"You hear it?" Draško stared at Gerasim, at Jude, seeking confirmation.

"Hear what!?" snapped Jude. He was listening now.

Draaaškoooooo

"Fuckin' that!" Draško screeched, throwing his hands over his ears, as the whisper became a banshee shriek, piercing his temporal lobe.

Gerasim and Jude flinched as Draško jumped up and lurched for the door and hammered on the thick wood, and hollered, "Matthias, please!" whacking it with every shrieked syllable, "I need the fuckin' toilet, man! I need the..." his words lost in a sob.

Draško banged the door twice more, spacing them apart.

"Your trousers? When did you pull them up?" Gerasim asked, noticing he was no longer catching sight of his friend's buttocks.

Puzzled by Ger's question, Draško turned to look at his friend... and smiled. "I don't need the toilet. Ger, I don't need the toilet," he laughed.

"Oh, the joy. The fuckin' joy," Jude drawled snidely.

But, with his hands on the door, his forehead resting against it, Draško didn't hear Jude's sarcasm.

Draaaškoooooo

Joy wouldn't be waiting for him.

10:24

"What the fuck am I doing?" Matthias questioned himself as he rapped on the basement door.

When the glass had moved along the mantel, untouched, it had freaked him out. The only people he could think were in the house were Jude and his pair of goons. *It couldn't be them,* he'd thought, as he'd made his way through the kitchen to the basement's concrete steps. He'd paused at the top. The blackness seeping up the stairs toward him was like a force pushing him away yet trying to draw him in simultaneously. The torchlight was weakening and only cast a meagre glow down the stairs. He stepped cautiously downward, following the flickering shadows.

He'd tried the door handle. The door was locked. Still locked. Crouching down, he sniffed the keyhole, and flinched and grimaced at the odour. Then he'd knocked on the door because, when there's a door, you either knock or you enter. And he had no desire to go in.

Flush-whoosh-clank-clang-gurgle-ting-ting-ping-rattle-rattle-groan...

The sound of the toilet flushing and water travelling through the old copper pipes and plumbing jarred him. He darted up the steps, through the kitchen and into the hallway.

Scrape-thud! Scrape-thud!

Shining the torch back to the staircase, Matt could see nothing but the flitting shadows and stains. But he heard it. He knew the sound.

Frantically, he shone the light up and down the hallway's two corridors, and around the foyer. Back-and-forth. Back-and-forth. But there was nothing but flickering shadows.

Silence.

As quickly as it had started, it stopped. The old farmhouse seemed to settle and breathe almost imperceptibly to itself. Matt stood still and listened. Nothing. Just his own deep breathing and his heartbeat thumping in his ears as his blood rushed around his body. *Just my heart and my breathing...* inhaling for three, hold, exhaling for three, hold, calming himself.

* * * * *

"Is this what you want?" Matthias muttered to the floor and walls and sofa in the living room, as he scribbled on the multicoloured Post-its.

Marker pen in his hand, he was driven by fear, seething with anger and agitation. He wasn't thinking at all. He felt his own breathing, tight and shallow. Felt as if his own eyes were bulging as the weak light cast colour and shade over the paper. Scribble-after-scribble, line-after-line, swirl-after-swirl. He frantically dragged the black pen across paper. Tearing off a note and discarding it onto the floor, making an ink mark on the next, before tearing that one off. Scribble and tear and discard. Scribble and tear and discard. Scribble, tear, discard.

The sounds that had jolted him and drawn him up from the basement moments ago began again. Flush-scrapethud-whoosh-scrapethud-clang-gurgle-scrapethud-ping-ting. They reverberated all around.

Matt began grabbing notes off the floor and sticking them against the wall. No discernible pattern, just pick-and-stick. Note after note. "Is this what you want, eh!?" He hollered up at the ceiling, at the walls of the living room, sticking note next to note. Bending, grabbing, sticking. Bending, grabbing, sticking. Bend-grab-stick. Bend-grab-stick. Quicker and quicker and quicker. His chest heaving, trying to take in air. Inhaling, exhaling, trying to breathe louder than the cacophony of sounds.

. . .

Then silence.

11:23

Jude reached into his top left pocket to retrieve his glasses.

They're not there. Nor is his pocket. Not really. Torn apart, hanging by its seams. And his jacket sits on him like a pile of dark, ripped rags. Slightly befuddled, he patted his hands around on the cold concrete floor, fumbling and feeling for his glasses in the dark, damp, cold basement.

Finding them, he puts them on. With only one arm, the glasses sit wonky on his nose, askew across his face. Adjusting the angle of them between finger and thumb so he can squint through a tiny shard of un-cracked lens, Jude takes in the room, and, somehow, through the blackness, he sees his Slavic guys, Gerasim and Draško - Gez and Dizzy, he calls them.

Draško scratched at the broken half of his face, finding only his gums and some of his jawbone where his teeth and cheek should've been. "It fuckin' itches', mate!" he moaned. "Aargh!" He angrily and frustratingly shoved a box across the concrete blackness, jumped up, hopped a few feet, and banged frantically on the basement door. "I need the fucking toilet!"

Gerasim looked to be struggling, too. His t-shirt collar ripped and torn across his throat, just across from his left shoulder. He's managed to hoick himself up into a sitting position using his hands and arms, but he's struggling to move his legs. "Stop moaning, Dras! No-one is hearing you," he reprimands his friend for his constant whinging.

"I don't like it in here, Ger. It is fuckin' haunted, man, I am telling you. You can hear that creaking and groaning outside… upstairs." he bangs on the door again.

Draško had hated confined spaces ever since that shop cellar back in Mostar. He had been okay for the first day and night and into the next day, but as soon as the nighttime darkness came again, he had started panicking. Screaming, shouting, wheezing, sweating, blinking. His IBS went through the roof… well, all over the floor. It was not good. Right now, he could feel the claustrophobic nausea creeping up on him, though he had no idea how long he'd been trapped in this cold, dark room.

"Get away from the door, Diz," growled Jude. "And pull your fucking trousers up."

Draško hopped and pigeon-stepped, crouched down to pull his trousers up, but he can't. "They won't come up, Jude. They're just stuck there, just -"

"Sit down."

"Matty can't keep us locked in here, Jude," Draško whined, turned, and stumbled as he thumped on the door again.

"Sit!" Jude barks.

"This is freaking me out! Ger!" Draško shouted back at Jude as he slid back down against the door.

"I heard you, buddy."

Of course, Gerasim knew why his friend was struggling. It had annoyed him back then, but they were young adolescents, so didn't fully understand the physical and mental side. Now they were older, Ger figured they ought to be stronger. It had been over twenty years, and he still found it annoying now. He would try to be tolerant of his friend.

"We heard you. Now give it a rest," Ger turned to Jude, "Just nerves, Jude -"

"It is not nerves. It is being locked in this fucking room. It is not right. It is not -"

"Dras. Dras. Calm down, friend. It will be okay, I'm telling…" Gerasim tried a more soothing, soft approach. But he was considering throwing his friend out of the basement, just like they had thrown Danika and Milena out.

But Draško really wasn't listening. He was complaining, "How the fuck did Matty get us in here? The gun… that was it. It wasn't the gun that we -" he stopped himself from blurting it out. He didn't want to get himself or Ger in trouble with Jude.

Gerasim gave a little look and nod of appreciation to his friend for the save.

"He forced us in here. But it was only you who had a -" Dras directed at Jude.

"Shut the fuck up! Sit down!" Jude bellowed, stopping Draško's whinge in its tracks.

Gerasim felt he knew what Draško was alluding to but didn't have the courage or the commitment to back his friend up. He figured if he went too far in Dras's defence, matters would escalate and would likely turn nasty. Besides, Jude had always looked out for the two of them, stuck up for them. He'd never let them down. He wanted to trust Jude now. Jude would sort it.

A rattle against the door.

Another rattle.

It's coming from the other side of the door, they're sure of it. Jude, Gerasim, and Draško exchange uneasy glances in their familiar yet distorted surroundings. Their unease hanging heavy in the stale air.

A third rattle. The door handle.

"It won't be okay. Okay? And I need the toilet." Draško twists and thumps on the door again.

There's a knock on the other side of the door.

Then another.

Disoriented, Draško, Gerasim, and Jude stare at each other.

"Matty!" shrieked Draško, "I need the toilet! Please!" giving the door two more whacks.

There's no repeat knock from the other side of the door.

E|L

I never saw   **never spoke**
                is there
                          alone
then not
                     matt is there not
there   purple
          nurturing nurturing
        embarazada **denial shook**   his
head in indignation

                  he lied **finger on the**
steel pistol
sale agreed **take me to the edge**
            i am liminal **black is white all i**
see is red   child heartbeat
heartbeat
                    leave it
for dead   **recoil**
from the backlash of what you said   house
sanctuary   **two**
       the front door   **lies**
yellow car   we are
liminal

58

arms hold me minutes
pass hours pass time is not linear its irregular four
metal sulphur what
is going on outside of your mind
nina nonata narcissist
man he loves me
he does not love me she to edify me six

not
coming home i am perdida the
red bus i feel
and i feel torment from deep within razor cuts blood

child stay down
just watching you bleed '
man in the glasses child heartbeat
heart
i can't breathe kiss her hair two cigarettes
pain

egomaniacal egomaniacal
egomaniacal concrete broken mirror

winter
nina nonato not venerable
i need to breathe speak to
the man nothing

matthias writing
creating for she me behind the
locked door of the big house handprint
handprint handprint handprint only when you feel so low
do your feelings show they are my dreams
i will dream them bleed
scream crawl to the stars give your soul so crawl phone

pinging and and

tobacco

voices in my head   eight distant muffled

colours rainbow ink ink   nine   you

speak deep in my heart   i wanted

everything with you eidolon

bodach

she was like water through my fingers   fingers

lies

12:22

The petrol can slid sideways in the passenger footwell, its contents sloshing, as the little yellow car turned into the property, its headlights lit up the SOLD sign outside the old farmhouse. The tyres crunched slowly to a halt on the old gravel that fronted the house.

The house that was to be their dream home.

Their forever home.

Matthias sat in the car for a moment, staring at the house. Anxious. Nervous. And with disbelief coursing through his mind, he really couldn't understand how she'd convinced him to come back here. There was nothing here for him. Not anymore. Nothing but painful memories, surreal events. The troubled thoughts niggled continuously through his head as he stepped out of the car into the thick night air, slinging the black rucksack over his shoulder.

His heart pounded in his chest as he pushed open the creaking door and stepped into the hallway foyer. Shadows danced to the light from his torch. The old bricks and wood and walls, the windows and floorboards and furniture seemed to breathe. He could feel the air brushing against his face, tickling his hair, coating him with a feeling of darkness. He could smell the stale, lingering scent of fear, of loss, mixed with tobacco and damp and dust and peeling wallpaper, and a sulphurous edge that crept up his nostrils and rattled his mind. It tasted metallic, palpable.

A wintery draught crept in under the doors and through the old windows, seeping through his clothes, giving him a chill that he could feel when the material touched his skin as his body trembled beneath his t-shirt, jacket and jeans. A shiver up his spine, a rattling in his chest, the wont to chatter his teeth. The metal of the torch casing cold in his hand. It was more than a draught.

He cast the weak torchlight around the hallway, sending shadows flicking and flittering around him. He shone the light past the dining room, seeing the old mahogany table upright but skew-whiff. exactly as he'd left it when... He snuffed out the spark of the memory.

He brought the light back around, past the living room, and toward the staircase. Raising the torch's beam slowly up the stairs and down again, the mix of light and dark shadow bouncing up and down on each step somehow made the stains on the carpet wriggle and twist, as if being conducted and choreographed by the torchlight before being thrust back into blackness as the light moved away.

Still standing by the front door, the old house groaned, cracked, and creaked, as Matthias moved the light back to the living room doorway, its door slightly ajar. It seemed foreboding, but it was the only room he knew he had to go in. About to take a step toward it, a movement to his left startled him, down the hallway corridor that led to the kitchen. He turned his head left and saw a tall, shadowy figure in the kitchen doorway. In the split second it took to shine the light down the corridor in the direction he was looking, the doorway was empty. Just the dark, shadowy shapes of the table and chairs. Did he see someone, something, or just imagine it?

Dismissing it - *who believes in ghosts?* - Matthias slowly pushed the living room door open. Its hinges creaked and moaned against the movement, having been unused for some time. The cloud-covered moonlight bleeding through the French doors gave the room an ethereal glow. Adding the torchlight to the incoming moonlight caused havoc and panic in the shadows, sending them skipping and jumping frantically around the room. It cast the old, ripped and torn leather armchair in light then dark, the handprint on the mirror flickering and jerking, giving it movement. The glass of water on the mantelpiece was cloudy and browning as it continued to erode the cigarette butt within.

And there, on the sofa - he couldn't say it, didn't want to think it - was the purple blanket. Exactly as he'd had left it.

He knew what he'd find here, but it didn't help mitigate the nausea in the pit of his stomach, or the weakness in his legs, or the pounding in his chest, or the shaking in his hands. The grief he'd been trying to deal with since he was last here was now clawing at his throat and his eyes and his lungs. He was more rattled than he thought he'd be. He took several steps backwards, dropped the rucksack onto the floor, and sat himself in the armchair. Bending forward, elbows on his knees, Matthias inhaled deeply and exhaled slowly until he felt a little steadier and calmer.

Raising his head, bringing his eyes up, attempting to look again at the purple shape in front of him, a glint of light caught his eye. Over by the sofa. His Zippo. He'd found it. He smiled a rare smile. It was the only thing, right then, that could make him move toward the sofa. He leant forward, kept his head bowed and his eyes on the silver. Pocketing it, the click against the lolly sticks both comforting and painful.

* * * * *

Eva wants to talk to you, she'd said. Write with passion, she'd said. Matt emptied the rucksack's consents, littering the floor with several pads of Post-it notes of yellow and green and blue and pink and orange and purple, and a black marker pen.

Write what? He stared at the sofa. *Write a song? A love note? Poetry? WHAT!?* Frustrated, angry, he kicked the coloured pads, scattering them across the floor. Some knocking the crushed cigar butt away, others bouncing off the bloodied skirting board.

"Write fucking what!?" Matt's angry words reverberated around the house.

The glass slowly slid and scraped along the mantel.

13:21

Days? Weeks?

Matthias wasn't sure how long it had been since he'd left her on the sofa. He'd been living on nothing but coffee. Well, he couldn't remember eating anything. And the taste of copious amounts of coffee was doing its best to mask the taste the house had left in his mouth, so he must have been living on the stuff, he reckoned.

He'd been thinking. Thinking some more. Overthinking it all. Drinking coffee. Thinking, drinking, overthinking. Chaos in his head. Yet he was still unsure of what to do, let alone how to do it. Unsure of how he could do anything. No amount of overthinking and coffee drinking could get him to the place in his mind where he was sure the solution lay dormant.

This late autumn morning, the early dawn's red, orange and gold hues had come glaring through the car windscreen and woken him. Disorientated and stiff and tired from sleeping upright and fitfully in the driver's seat of Eva's little yellow car, he'd scratched his newly grown beard, stretched to loosen his aching and sore back and shoulders, urinated in the nearby hedge, and wandered the paths around the lakes, blurred by a haze of exhaustion and emotion. Still wearing the same clothes he was wearing days ago, or was it weeks ago? They were sweaty and grimy and clung to him in places they shouldn't.

Tired, exhausted, dragging his feet, Matthias stepped onto the little wooden bridge. He still felt like he couldn't breathe. He hadn't smoked since his last conversation with Jude. He was thinking about smoking now. He pulled the silver cigarette case out, popped it open, and looked at the single cigarette. He patted himself down, looking for his Zippo. Couldn't find it. Gave up, snapped the case closed, and put it back in his pocket.

He doubted he'd buy any more cigarettes, so best to have that one when he could savour the moment.

Hunched up against the cold morning breeze, Matt put his hands in his jacket pockets, trying to warm up. The rough, dirty wool of the jacket pinched against his cold hands. He felt the shape and cold metal of the basement key nestled amongst the loose collection of lolly sticks. He didn't want to think about the key, and he moved his fingers a little and the rough wood of the lolly sticks stung his cold fingers as the hew rubbed against them. He pulled out two sticks and smiled wistfully. Leaning over the handrail, ready to play a solitary game of pooh sticks, Matt paused, reached into his pocket, snapped a lolly stick in half, and put one half with the other two, and dropped them into the stream.

He wouldn't get to see which came out first on the other side.

"I know why you come here, Matthias." Gravelly, Spanish patois, to his right.

He turned his head to see Alma standing at the curve of the bridge. Her dark eyes, framed by her long, black hair, squared off fringe, a black rucksack slung over her right shoulder. Her three-piece tailored navy-blue suit and lilac silk pocket square was at odds with her bare feet.

He turned his back to her and walked away in the opposite direction.

Alma called after him, "I not going away, Matthias. I will keep coming... this time and again... no matter how long time it takes. I know when you come here, Matthias." Alma made her way to where he was standing, watched him exit the bridge, and step down the bank to the stream. "I know is... how you say? Weird."

"Weird doesn't explain it at all, Alma! The fuck're you doing here!?" Matthias hollered, picking up some stones from the ground, not looking at her at all, choosing to skim a couple of stones across the stream.

"It's been some time, Matthias. You must trade. You must deal with -"

Matt looked up at her, "Fuck off, Alma. Trade what? Deal? How am I supposed to deal with it, eh!? You think I haven't been trying? Thinking... thinking... it's all I'm fuckin' doing! And how the fuck do you -"

"Vete al infierno bastardo egoista. Estás atrapado en un momento. Sólo tú puedes cambiar las cosas. Solo tú puedes ayudarnos a todas a seguir adelante. Así que lidia con eso!" Alma shrieked down from the bridge, her temper fraying a little. "Time heals the wounds, Matthias." She adds more calmly.

"Time heals fuck all, Alma!" he hurled another stone into the stream.

Alma's presence was the last thing he wanted. Or expected. He didn't like her. Her being here, in this place he once cherished, made him feel uneasy. Why had she come here?

She'd crossed the rest of the bridge and was now standing at the top of the bank. "You know what my name it is say in English?" she asked calmly.

Matt furrowed his brow in confusion. "What!? Your name!? It's Alma... so I say Alma", pointing an exaggerated finger at his mouth as he sounded out her name, before repeating the sarcasm, "Watch my lips: Alma."

Alma kissed her teeth and threw her hands up in frustration. She turned her back on Matthias, looked up to the sky, and said,

"¿Realmente debo seguir hablando con este hombre? ¿Debo ayudarlo? Es un maldito idiota. Estúpido. Nunca entenderé por qué lo amas, mi bella reina." She turned back to face him. "No, Matthias, all of my name. Is Alma Sofia."

Matt was certain she'd called him an idiot and stupid. But he didn't understand any other part of it.

"You know this meaning?" she asked a second time.

Aggravated by her, his animosity grew, and he took a step toward her, "That your name is Alma Sofia." Matt scoffed sarcastically back at her.

"It is meaning... I don't know how to say in English. What English is for..." she lifted her hands up either side of her face, opened her eyes wide, waggled her fingers, and gave an exaggerated, piercing, "Wooo!"

Matt counts the black rings visible on her left hand's fingers, *Two, four... six, eight...nine -*

"Wooo," Alma stepped closer to Matt and repeated her sounds and hand waving.

Distracted, Matt laughed and mimicked her hand movements. "Wooo... Wooo. Does it mean jazz hands? The wind blowing in the trees?" he scoffed and started to walk away.

"Gilipollas!" Alma shook her head in frustration. "Significa que soy sabia y puedo hablar con los espíritus," then bowed her head to one side, as if listening. "Puedo hablar con Eva"

Matt stopped, "What?" he questioned, stunned at hearing her name.

"¿Cómo puedo hacer que entienda esto?" Alma whispered to herself.

Turning to face Alma, leaning his head forward, he quietly and pointedly asked, "What? What the fuck are you saying to me, Alma?" He felt his heart rate rise. Not angry. Not upset. Agitated.

"Eva is want you go back to the house, Matthias. I talk her."

For a moment, he could do nothing but stare at Alma. Then he turned back and stared at the stream, no longer wanting to be absorbed into her dark eyes. He swallowed back the tears that were coming. "Go back!? Go back!? I can't go back there. You don't think I've thought about anything else for... I don't know how long... days, weeks?" his voice cracked. Choking, he quietly added, "I can't. I'm done. I'm numb, Alma. Fuckin' numb... empty"

"El vacío es un sentimiento... pero puedes seguir adelante. Debe haber perdón en todos lados. Cierre." Alma steps closer to Matthias, "Eva is need see you."

A sense of unease washed over Matthias, mingling with the tendrils of hope that should not be there, as Alma extended the rucksack towards him.

"You must write, Matthias. Escribe con fuego. Write with passion," she pleaded with him, and gave the rucksack a forceful shake, emphasising it, and the importance of his taking it.

With some trepidation, Matt accepted the rucksack. Its true weight was as if it held no contents, yet he felt it heavy against his grip and he had to let his arm drop to his side, the bottom of the rucksack touching the stony, crisp, dewy ground.

He turned away from Alma, found his way back onto the footpath, and, dragging the rucksack by his side, Matthias walked away.

R|A

i speak with her

take the path

matt is there

alone

then not alone the woman with the

purple

nurturing

embarazada **denial shook**   his

head

insanity inside of my head i am liminal

child heartbeat

heartbeat

the lakes   recoil
from the backlash   **the bridge** the house
                              smells of coffee two

yellow car   we are
liminal   **sobbing**

tell me talk to me   minutes
pass hour hours   **time is not linear** its irregular **four**
                                    what is
going on outside of your mind
                nina nonata
man comes home   he loves   woman please come
home   **she to edify me six**

coming home i am   **destiny fate** perdida
                                its hard to bear
        i feel torment from deep within

                                child heartbeat
heartbeat
i can't breathe   **two cigarettes**
                                    pain

concrete broken mirror

                        winter venerable man

i need to breathe   **speak to the man**
                saw you there always there
                                matthias writing
creating for she me   behind the
locked door of the big house
                only when you feel so low do
your feelings show   they are my dreams i will
dream them
    to the stars give your

and and

eight

ink ink   **nine i need to hear you speak**

                                i wanted

          everything with you eidolon

bodach   she was

like water through my fingers

                              she wants to meet

me

14:20

Matthias pulled back the purple blanket and knelt to kiss her soft, still warm, blotchy face, tracing the contours of her cheeks, her nose, her chin, her ears. Twiddling her hair. She liked it when he twiddled her hair as she snuggled up under the blanket.

"I'm so, so sorry, Eva," he said softly, placing his hand across her chest. "I... I told them, didn't I? I told them what I'd do if anything happened to you...you remember?"

The night had drawn in and the only light enabling him to see was the moonlight creeping in through the French doors. But he didn't want to see any more. Stealing this one kiss, he rolled the blanket back to cover her up.

"Go see your mum, babes."

Matt's chest heaved, trying to draw a deep breath, but the living room felt heavy and airless, and all he could inhale into his nose, his throat, his lungs, was a mix of gunpowder, stale tobacco smoke, dust, and despair.

He needed to breathe.

The garden was a welcome sanctuary, a blissful supply of fresh, cold air, and stepping out through the French doors, Matthias breathed deeper than he'd probably ever done before. He placed his hands in his pockets, bracing against the late evening chill, and he fingered the cold metal of the basement key. He'd need to keep hold of that, he guessed.

Then he felt the weight and cold of the gun. He didn't want it.

He wandered through the garden. He'd wanted to walk this garden with Eva. Work the garden with her. Plant plants. Grow veg. Pick the fruit from the trees in the late summer. All of it with her.

None of that would happen now.

The air was still, and an autumn mist was gathering over the garden. Matthias walked in search of the ornamental pond. It was too dark and too misty to see the water, but mist was more prevalent over water, so it acted as his guide. With a splosh, he dropped the gun into the shallow water. Too dark and too misty to see the ripples.

He did not know what he should do now or next. He stared back toward the darkness of the house. Stared around the misty garden. Stared up at the clear, dark sky, taking in the moon. Thinking, thinking, thinking. Thinking about her, water, the living room, bathroom, fireplace, dining room, mirror, kitchen, table, the sofa, the blanket, the basement, Jude, Grim, Dung, concrete, walls, blanket, sofa.

Blanket.

Sofa.

Eva.

And.

He didn't know what he should do now. But he knew what he shouldn't do. Or rather, could not do. He could not stay in the house. Not right now. Maybe not for a long time.

He needed to breathe.

He needed to think.

15:19

The scent of gun smoke and tobacco still lingered in the air as Matt stepped back into the living room.

Straight ahead, in front of the French doors, Jude was still slumped in the leather wingback armchair. This was Eva's father. Perhaps he should be a bit more respectful; more careful than he was with Grim and Dung. Then again, he was the reason for all this shit, wasn't he?

Matthias stood and stared and pondered for a long minute, agitated.

Fuck him!

He grabbed Jude's ankles and yanked him off the chair, slamming his head onto the floor, just missing the crushed cigar. The impact of Jude's head on the floor, sent his glasses tumbling from his face, yet he'd not totally cleared chair - Jude's right arm was still draped up in the chair's seat. Irritated, Matt stamped on the glasses, snapping an arm off and cracking the remaining good lens. He then placed the glasses in his own top pocket and resumed to drag Jude clear of the armchair, the right arm flopping down and slapping against the floor and bouncing up against the wall.

The sweat and blood on Jude's right hand and fingers left a bloodied streak and an accompanying squeak along the length of the skirting board, as Matt dragged Jude from the living room.

Practically launched down the basement's concrete steps, Jude cracked and squelched as he hit the basement door. Matt stepped on him to get into the darkness and dragged him roughly over the damp, rough floor, shoving him violently against the wall.

When leaving the basement, Matt launched Jude's glasses into the pitch black, roughly in the direction he thought Jude was.

The basement door creaked closed, and Matthias locked it and put the key in his pocket, and made his way up the steps, his hands on the wall either side to guide him up.

One, two, three.

Done.

16:18

Grim hadn't moved.

He was lying behind the dining room table in a pool of blood. The bullet had ripped right through his collarbone and throat and bedded itself into the wall adjoining the kitchen. Matthias had to move the table before he could move Grim. A lot of effort went into lifting the old mahogany dining table back upright and sliding out of the way. It was a heavy lump of wood.

"Grim, Grim, Grim. How the fuck did you think you could throw that at me?" Matt puffed and he bent down to grab Grim's armpits.

Dragging Grim through the house left a trail and smear and splatter of blood. But he cracked and crunched and squelched with the same sound as his friend when Matt rolled him down the concrete steps to the basement.

From what he could make out through touch alone in the basement's dark, Matt left Grim draped over his friend's legs.

Two down.

One to go.

17:17

Matthias found Dung five steps up.

He'd clearly survived for a little while after being dragged downstairs. His trousers were still down by his ankles, his bare backside mooning at Matthias. Dried excrement stuck to his buttocks gave off an unpleasant reek.

"You smelly, dumb fuck, Dung. Why crawl back upstairs? Needed the toilet again? The front door is right there. You wouldn't have made it, sure, but you might've nearly got there. Hey, who knows, I might've found you face down in the driveway, with gravel stuck up your nose and in your mouth. It would've been less fucking effort that pulling your half naked, shit-stained self up the stairs."

Straining to see what he was doing as the house darkened as the evening drew in, Matt hooked Dung's ankles under his arms and pulled him down the steps at a pace - scrapethud scrapethud scrapethud scrapethud - Dung's body dragged against the floor, his head bumping down each step. Scrape-Thud! Bouncing him onto the hallway floor. Dragging and scraping him across the foyer, turning right, past the dining room, through the kitchen, banging him into the chairs.

Matt paused at the top of the concrete steps that led into the basement. It was a pitch black, dark void. No light was coming up from there. And what fading evening light there was coming in through the kitchen window was not penetrating beyond the first two steps.

He dragged Dung to the top step. Pushed hard, and watched the body disappear into the void, hearing bones crunch and crack and squelch. Then fall silent. Dung had reached the basement door.

Treading slowly and carefully, Matthias made his way down to the basement, stopping when his feet hit something firm but with a bit of fleshy give. Fumbling in the dark, he found the key and unlocked the door, twisted the handle, and shoved the old wooden door inwards. The smell of damp and dust and brick and wood and age hit him full-on, making him flinch, turn his head away and let out a loud exhale of breath.

Sliding Dung over the damp concrete floor, Matthias left him sitting up against some old boxes.

One down.

Two to go.

18:16

The air in the living room hung heavy with the acrid scent of gunpowder and the metallic tang of blood, mixing with fresh tobacco.

Matthias had stood stock still and stared for what felt like forever but must have been much less because he felt his cigarette burning between his fingers, jolting him out of this trance. He sucked his tongue through a sharp intake of breath, in reaction to the sting, stepped over to the mantel and dropped his cigarette into the glass of water. The short pfft sound as the ember fizzled out, pushing up a very short wisp of smoke as its life was snuffed out. *Oh, the irony*, he thought.

He couldn't turn away from the mantel. The only thing he dared to cast his eyes at was his own reflection in the Regency mirror. *I look like shit!* he thought. *Not very descriptive for a writer.* His eyes' sclera red, his hair floppy, sweaty, and dark circles were appearing under his eyes. His blue irises were now closer to a faded grey. He looked fifty-eight instead of twenty-eight.

When he could no longer look at himself, he stared deeper into the mirrored glass and stared at the reflection of the purple blanket on the sofa. "Damn it, Eva," Matt whispered, his voice carrying a mixture of anguish and disbelief. "This wasn't supposed to happen. We were supposed to have a life together."

His quiet, one-way conversation with Eva was interrupted by a message notification. It wasn't his phone. It was Eva's. It gave him a reason to turn away from the mirror and take in the reality that lay on the sofa. There, on the floor, was her phone.

The cracked screen had automatically lit up on receipt of the message.

It was from Alma.

'**Hey babes**...' the auto preview showed. But that was all he could glean from the locked screen.

He also saw the notifications stating three missed calls and two voicemails. He knew they were from him.

He didn't give a fuck what Alma wanted, and he didn't need to listen to the voicemails because he remembered exactly what he had said. How he would have happily waited to see her, if he'd known what he'd find when he got here.

On his knees, his head resting on the blanket, not really sure what to do at that moment, Matthias simply slid the phone under the sofa. Out of sight, out of mind.

He stayed there until late afternoon became early evening. If he'd looked behind him, he would have seen the sun setting through the French doors, the twilight changing the tone of the garden, and throwing the living room into an even darker canvas.

19:15

Jude, glass of water in his left hand - still trying to rid himself of the dryness in his throat, his furry tongue - glanced into the dining room on his right as he made his way from the kitchen to the living room, seeing a terrified Gez facing down the barrel of Matty's gun.

He knew Matty had seen him out of the corner of his eye.

As composed as Jude was trying to be, his heart was racing, and his legs had turned to jelly. He felt himself wobble even further as he entered the living room and passed Eva's body on the sofa. That he only saw the purple blanket didn't ease matters. He made his way to the marble fireplace, took a gulp of water, and placed the half-empty glass on the mantelshelf. He flinched at the sound of the gunshot, placing his sweaty, bloody, greasy right hand on the mirror, trying to steady himself against the gravity of the situation.

Two for one. Maybe Matty'll take that, he thought, trying to reconcile matters in his own favour.

He could feel Matty standing in the doorway. Raising his eyes, Jude checked his own reflection. He looked done in, finished. Somehow, he felt his cracked lens was symbolic of how broken he was; how broken this whole thing was. But he refused to believe it. Looking beyond his own image, deeper into the mirror, he could see Matty take a step into the living room, gun in his right hand, bouncing shakily against his thigh.

"What can I say? What do you want me to say?" Jude asked rhetorically, sliding the glass along the mantelshelf, left-to-right, and stepping toward the leather armchair, leaving his grimy, sweaty and blooded handprint stain on the mirror.

Jude flopped into the chair and removed his cracked glasses, pointed them toward the sofa. His face screwed up in anguish, his eyes tear up, his bottom lip quivers, and his chest rises and falls repeatedly as he fights the oncoming sobs.

"I am sorry... truly sorry," he said, not knowing if he was saying it to Matty or to his daughter. Or even if he really meant it. Deep down, he knew he was most likely saying it to himself. He took out a cigar from his top pocket and popped it between his teeth, thinking that he's definitely more likely apologising to himself for this situation. He pats himself down, looking for a lighter. He can't find one.

Awkward.

Matthias approached Jude slowly. Taking his Zippo out, he offered the flame up to the cigar. Jude dragged and puffed, dragged and puffed, until the cigar lit, and took a big inhale of the thick smoke. He held his breath for a few seconds before he exhaled. The burning tobacco partially masked the decaying odour of the room.

Matthias, his hands shaking, retreated two steps from Jude and opened his cigarette case. Two cigarettes remained. He took one out and held it between his lips. Trying to light it, the gun made it awkward. He fumbled and dropped his Zippo, sending it bouncing across the wooden floor. He didn't see where it ended up. And it wasn't the moment for him to scrabble around trying to find it.

Awkward.

Jude returned the favour by offering his glowing cigar. A hesitant two steps forward, Matthias used it to spark up his cigarette. He then retreated two steps.

In silence, the two men savoured their tobacco and nicotine. Matt still bouncing the gun against his thigh.

"She shouldn't have been there, Jude

"I said no guns, Matty. Where the fuck did you get a gun?"

"What!? The gun's got fuck all to do with it, Jude!"

Jude felt the weight of Matty's words. Though he was slowly resigning himself to this moment, accepting it was the right thing, he would not accept that he was at fault. "You called her."

Three missed calls. "She shouldn't have been there!" Matt shot back at Jude.

"She was distracted by her phone, Matty! She forgot what she was supposed to be doing, and it all went to shit. The job was going clean, like clockwork, on schedule. Just like we all agreed. There was no trouble... then you called her. You. Called. Her. You killed her."

"Wh - What? What... why are you saying that? Don't... don't fuckin' try to put this on me, Jude! It was your deal. The condition you put on her. On us!" Matt is hit by the word *condition*. "It's all fucking gone. Lives gone! You wanted this for her -"

"You think I wanted this for my daughter? For my daughter!? Fuck off!" Jude croaked, his voice gruff and burdened with the guilt and sadness he felt, but more by the disbelief that he was in this situation. His narcissism and stubbornness wouldn't let himself show it or admit it, especially not to Matty. "Put it in one of your fucking stories -" Knowing he would not say another word, all his grief, anger and venom delivered, "Matty!"

Matthias pointed the gun at Jude.

"It's fuckin' Matthias. My name is Matthias!"

"We don't need to do this, Matty. We don't. You've taken my boys. I've given up Gez and Diz. Two for one. Is that not enough? It doesn't need to go further. You know it won't bring her back. It won't bring you anything, Matty. It's done... just let me walk out of here and you'll never see me again -"

"Like you let Eva's mother walk out? You're a narcissistic cunt, Jude. A cunt! You fuckin' killed her. You fuckin' killed 'em both. Killed Grim and Dung. Fucked it all up. I've got fuckin' nothin'. Nothin'!"

Jude leant forward with a snarl on his face. He knew he wasn't getting out of the chair, the house. He was not getting out of this situation at all. "Well, she can go see her mum now, can't she! All girls together!" he spat, dropped his cigar and crushed it onto the wooden floor at the foot of the armchair.

20:14

The gunshot echoed through the farmhouse.

Gerasim had almost jumped out of his skin when Jude had entered the kitchen moments earlier, putting his fingers to his lips for him to be quiet. He had poured himself a glass of water. The adrenaline and trauma of this afternoon's events had dried his mouth out. He watched as Jude drew a glass of water from the tap and gulped it down in one go. He then poured a second glass, took a second small sip, and placed it on the draining board next to Gerasim's.

Cowering in the kitchen with Jude, a kind of safety in numbers thing, made Ger feel awkward and uncomfortable. Jude had always been strong; he'd been good to them. But Jude cowering in here with him was very out of character. He, himself, nervous, scared, did not sit comfortably in his own skin, his own mind. Normally, he and Jude and Draško would have stood up to anyone, fronted-up to them. But this time, this felt different. It was not a situation he'd ever faced. And he'd never faced one this personal.

The air in the kitchen hung thick with tension as both Jude and Gerasim had flinched the split-second they heard the visceral sound of the gun, knocking over one of the two glasses of water resting on the draining board, and raising their eyes to the ceiling.

It was the sixth time Gerasim had heard close-range gunshots in his life. They'd had shooters on previous jobs they'd done with Jude, but they'd never had to use them. But, as a child, back in his homeland, he'd heard pockets of erratic gunfire as troops moved through the town and surrounding areas. But they were not what he called 'real gunshots' - specific gunshots, ones with purpose. This one was. The fourth of the day; three from the job earlier, and now this one. The previous two times had been when he and Draško had sent the insolent Danika out of the shop cellar into the clutches of the waiting squad of soldiers. Gerasim's sister, Milena, had followed. He'd not stopped her. About an hour after the girls had fled the cellar, he and Draško heard the two gunshots. Stupid bitches, he'd thought.

He'd got a piece so that he, or maybe Draško, could make Matty pay for his rude impudence about the smell of Dras's bum on the blanket. Not so Matty could turn the tables on them. Wait. Draško ditched the pigeon when they'd got out to pick up Eva -

Eva, the cause of all this trouble, this bad luck. He knew they should have left her to die in the road. She deserved it. But now his friend was... was... he didn't know, for sure.

"Oh, shit, Jude! Not Dras! No. Fuck!" exclaimed Gerasim, holding tight to the back of one of the kitchen chairs to support his nervous, anxious, unsteady self. He looked over to Jude, whose stare was trying to penetrate the ceiling, as if he was trying to see what was happening upstairs.

Where the fuck did you get a gun from, Matty? The thought put the fear into Gerasim. He'd been worried, a little scared, perhaps, about how Matty might react. But Matty reacting with a gun was a different matter altogether. *Jude said no guns.*

Scrape-thud! Scrape-thud! Scrape-thud!

Scrapethud-scrapethud-scrapethud... scrape-thud!

"Fuck! Fuck! Jude!" Gerasim panicked.

Scrape-thud!

Scrape-thud!

"C'mon, Jude, we've got to go, boss. Now!" Gerasim hollered, staring out of the kitchen, down the empty arm of the hallway leading to the front door. He didn't know what was stopping him. Did he need Jude's permission? Was Jude coming?

Scrape-thud!

Scrape-thud!

Jude stood stock-still. The only change was that his gaze was now straight out of the kitchen doorway, down the hallway, to the front door. But he clearly wasn't thinking about moving.

Scrape-thud.

Gerasim clearly didn't feel the same as Jude and couldn't wait any longer for his decision or permission, so he thrust himself away from the chair, sending it clattering to the linoleum floor, and darted from the kitchen into the long arm of the hallway. Adrenaline and the heightened need for flight rather than fight made him unsteady on his feet. The front door was just twenty-five feet away. A long, long twenty-five feet.

Scrape-

He stumbled past the dining room to his right, throwing out his arms and hands to use the walls to stop him from falling. He made it to the hallway foyer. The front door was now just a few feet away. Then to his left -

Thud!

Creak-

Gerasim should have ignored the sounds. And when something entered his peripheral vision, he shouldn't have looked to his left, toward the stairs. But he did. He wished he hadn't. He didn't want to see what he saw -

Matty stood at the bottom of the stairs, holding the left leg of a blood-covered Draško.

Gerasim might have been able to reach the front door. To open it. But he'd have to pause his momentum to grab the handle, turn it and pull the large, heavy door. And he didn't want to stop moving. He turned on his heels to dart back in the direction he'd come from. The kitchen? Jude loomed large in the kitchen doorway. *Jude? Jude... Come on, do something. Let me back in. Why won't you let me back? Help me.* The dining room, now on his left, was his only option. His only refuge.

Slamming the door shut behind him, childish reflex made him dive for cover behind the old, grand, mahogany dining table, close his eyes and cover his head - if I can't see him, he can't see me. Despite his heavy breathing and his heart hammering in his ears, he heard the creak of the hallway's worn floorboards.

The dining room door crashed open.

Opposite to the expected reflex, Gerasim's eyes opened, and he turned his head toward the sound of the door being flung open. He could see tan-coloured worker boots. Specs and splatters of blood staining the suede. Then he realised the table provided him no cover at all. A futile attempt to hide. *Shit!* With a burst of surprising energy, driven by the need to protect himself, to survive, Gerasim launched upward, grabbed the edge of the table and flipped it up and over towards his assailant.

But it all happened slow motion.

It all went wrong.

The old table was heavy and didn't move any distance at all, simply toppling over onto its side, sheltering Gerasim's legs but leaving his upper half fully exposed.

An easy target for the gun now pointed at him.

21:13

Flush. Whoosh. Clank. Clang. Gurgle. Ting. Ting. Ping. Rattle. Rattle. Groan.

The aging toilet and pipes and plumbing orchestra played loudly in the bathroom and reverberated round the house. There was no hiding that someone had been to the toilet. It could not be an inconspicuous function. Not in this house. Everyone would know where you'd been. And how long you'd been there.

From the moment Jude had darted out from behind the Post Office counter, to being here in the farmhouse toilet had been a blur. *Had Jude gone back on his word? Had he lied? Was it him? What bad luck had the witch brought down on them?* Draško could not make sense of anything. His guts shook and rattled.

Sat there on the toilet, his thoughts remained on the Eva trouble. He should have refused to have a woman involved. He should have cast her out, just like he did Danika. Eva had laughed at him, at his affliction, just like Danika had all those years ago. Even back then, though just a boy, he'd been angry and brave enough to throw a girl out for making him feel stupid. He wished he'd been strong enough this time, but he didn't know how Jude would react. And he didn't want to face an angry Jude. His stomach and bowels churned and griped at this thought.

His guts had been a problem ever since he was a child. He always had to know where the nearest toilet was. As he'd gotten older, girls were attracted to him right up to the point the IBS became the only subject of conversation. His adult relationships, more often than not, started with a little sympathy and understanding of his condition, but soon they all became tinged with subtle ridicule, before transitioning into piss-taking, right before intolerance set in forcing the relationship to end. All he could do, here in modern England, was to give them a slap as a parting gift. There wasn't a squad of armed and angry soldiers to do his dirty work for him.

Feeling his bowels were easing, he stood in front of the toilet bowl, trousers round his ankles, head bowed, making sure the flush had emptied the bowl. Hoping that it wouldn't need a second flush. And hoping that his stomach and arse would settle down and stop their griping. He needed to be with Gerasim. He was sobbing and muttering to himself, pleading to his friend, "Oh, Ger, Ger. What happened, friend? Oh, fuck, man! I don't know... I don't know! Why hadn't Eva opened the fucking car doors quicker!? Stupid witch! And fuckin' Jude, man!"

The antiquated water system settled down, the noise abating. Only to be replaced by stomping and creaking on the stairs. Dizzy swivelled his head to face the bathroom door. He stood absolutely still. Not breathing.

A second passed.

Another second.

If only he'd not ditched the pigeon shooter Gerasim had got for them.

Another.

Nothing happened.

Draško bent down to pull up his boxers and trousers up -

Crash!

The door flew open. Its old hinges failing to suppress the force, so the door violently smashed against the old enamel bath, cracking the rim, and wedging itself in place.

Stunned by the noise and the violence, Draško dropped his underwear and trousers back around his ankles.

Framed by the empty doorway, right in front of him, stood Matthias, his face contorted with anguish, his eyes wet and raging, his breathing ragged.

And he was pointing a gun straight at the centre of Draško's face.

I ditched it. That's not mine. I don't understand. Jude threw his away. He ditched it! "Matty, Matty, please. Please. Not in the toilet, Matty. Not -"

22:12

Unsure why, once he strode from his car and through the open front door, Matthias slowed within three small steps, slammed the front door shut, stopped in the centre of the hallway foyer, and listened.

The house was quiet. Not silent, but eerily quiet. Too quiet for a house with people in. Four people. There should be some disturbance of air, some muttering of voices. Breathing. Something.

He heard wheezing, rasping, gasping coming from the living room.

Cautiously, hesitantly, Matthias stepped into the room, the door creaking as it opened wider. The late afternoon sun's rays came in through the French doors, illuminating the recently disturbed dust particles, making them slightly visible as they danced in the otherwise muted pallor of the dark and grey room.

Looking around quickly, his eyes adjusted to the dim and shadowy room in a couple of seconds. He immediately wished they hadn't. He wanted to be blind. He didn't want to see what he was seeing. He physically felt his heart miss a beat and his stomach drop as he took in the sight of her laid out on the sofa. The state of her overalls, the mess of the bottom half of her body, the blood staining her lips, chin, nose. The rasp of her shallow breaths failing to give rise and fall to her chest. He was seeing it.

Please. No. It isn't. It can't be. Matthias stumbled forward and fell to his knees next to her broken body, lying supine. He grabbed her blotchy hand, placed his head on her chest.

"Eva... please," Matt choked through his quivering lips, fighting back tears and sobs. He clung to her, trying to stave off the inevitable. "Please stay with me".

Matt, I'm here. Matt? I'm in so much pain. Please help me. What happened to me? I don't know. I can't move. Hold my hand. Please. I can't catch my breath. I can't breathe.

Though hardly audible, Eva's laboured, shallow, coarse breath was deafening to him. He could feel her struggle, her pain. "I love you I love you I love you I love you I love you... please please please..." he pleaded, his face inches above hers.

Her eyes were blank, an unfocused stare. Not even a distant glimmer in her dilated pupils. A teary glaze fading the colour of her irises. Her lips purple-blue, blood-stained teeth displayed as her mouth slowly dropped open as muscles relaxed.

I love you so much, Matt. Help me, please. I can't see. I can't breathe.

The lump in Matt's throat felt severe, his watery eyes making Eva a blurry vision. The ache in his jaw - from clenching his teeth, trying to prevent a flood of tears - pummelled his temples with pain.

The pain, Matt, it's going. It's going... help me now, please. I need to breathe. I can't breathe. I'm frightened, Matt. Are you still there? I'm cold. I'm cold, Matt.

As though he could hear her, Matthias laid the purple blanket over her, resting it below her chin. She always took comfort from the blanket. Maybe, somehow, she'd get some succour from it now.

Get it out of my mouth, Matt! It tastes horrible! It tastes like copper. Your cologne. I can smell you. I can smell old wood... leather... dust. Matt, Matt!

Matt dropped back on his haunches, his left hand resting on Eva's belly. He knew the unavoidable was just a moment away. She was leaving him now. And And.

I'm so, so cold. Black… plastic… gun… door… phone. He lied. A phone. My phone. Ringing… wheels… Matt. Matt. I'm so cold, Matt. I want my mum. Mum! I can't breathe anymore. No more. Breathe for me, Matt.

Eva hadn't drawn another breath.

Matthias paused for what felt like an eternity to take in a last look at her face before closing her drooping eyelids and covering her fully with the blanket. He was alone now. He had no one else. No dreams. No future. His life that would never be swam around him, drowning him.

Matthias threw his head back and wailed. Wailed with loss, despair, sadness.

He wailed with anger.

S|N

i speak

matt is there

writing for me   alone

not alone

purple

denial

in indignation

pistol weighed heavy

steal steal steal

insanity inside of my head i am liminal

silver silver silver glints and sparkles   heartbeat

leave it for

dead   recoil from

the backlash of what you said   the house

i love you

door slams   lies   secrets

we are liminal

glass shattered splintered

writing

tell me talk to me
time is not linear its irregular
rheumy sclera dust metal sulphur fire what is going on
outside of your mind   i am floating
                looking for narcissist man comes
home charred he loves   woman please come home
                she to edify me   **shrieking at the men**
murmuration of starlings   not **coming**
home i   **destiny fate perdida**
the land is not green and fair its hard to bear   i
feel torment from deep within

                                    decaying

rooms
just watching you bleed   **man**
in the glasses   the **child** heartbeat

                            i can't breathe kiss
her   **cigarette**s

                pain   no more

                                            the
girl cold   egomaniacal   concrete
broken mirror   words
spoken   **winter** venerable man
not venerable outside   love is thrown **i need to**
breathe flicker flame   **speak to the man**
            saw you there
                matthias writing creating for she me
                behind the locked door of the big
house   handprint **handprint** handprint
handprint **only when you feel so low do your feelings show**
            they are my dreams i will dream them
scream of swifts now youre gone **bleed scream crawl**
        give your soul

and and remember better days
        tobacco   turmoil **the soil**   voices in my
head tears it apart   **colours rainbow**
ink ink ink   **taste** nine   **you speak**
            i wanted
        eidolon can you hear me calling
bodach clink   **rasp**

youre everywhere except here   clunk
        closure closure closure
    born a million lies

23:11

It was the day of Jude's deal, his condition.

Matthias tried to fill his day with writing and drinking coffee, and watching the clock, writing and drinking coffee and watching the clock. Rinse and repeat. And, on quite a few occasions, he'd opened his cigarette case and stared longingly at the two remaining cigarettes. But he'd resisted the temptation.

It wasn't about him. Today was about Eva being done with her old ways, her old life.

It was now coming up to quarter-past-three in the afternoon, and he was feeling his annoyed and agitated feeling. And worried. Worried he'd not heard from Eva. She had said the job would be done by three and, despite the no phones rule, she'd drop him a text as soon as they were away and heading over to the farmhouse.

She'd not been best pleased when he'd tried to 'track her down' when she'd been to see Alma the other day. Caring isn't always sharing, so it seems. He'd tried to make light of it, but it took a good day-or-so for her to see it from his side. Well, kind of see it.

Bollocks to it! He called her phone. Let it ring a few times. No answer. He hung up and decided to make himself a coffee. Maybe another cup would calm his mind. Kettle on, he opened the top cupboard to get himself a cup and saw the gun. Suddenly, he felt very anxious. He figured he'd forget the coffee and head over to the farmhouse. Besides, he was looking forward to seeing the house again, and seeing Eva most of all.

Thinking that his concern was down to overthinking, but still carrying enough anxiety and doubt due to what day this actually was, he grabbed the gun, picked up Eva's purple blanket and left the house and jumped into Eva's little yellow car.

The mid-afternoon sun dipped lower on the horizon as Matt navigated through Renborough, emergency vehicle sirens providing an unwanted soundtrack, adding to his growing anxiety. He directed the little car out toward the countryside, on his way towards the old farmhouse. His anxiousness grew with every passing mile, with every minute his phone didn't ring or ping. The autumn afternoon sun cast long shadows across the road, eerily shaped shadow after eerily shaped shadow flickered light and dark across his field of vision. He dialled Eva's number, his heart fluttering with the eagerness to hear her voice.

The ringtone echoed in the car's interior, a haunting contrast to the serene countryside. As the call connected, Matt's voice exuded a warmth that belied the turmoil unfolding in his mind.

"Hey, Evie, babes, how's it going? Everything okay? You done? I've not heard from you, so just a call from me to you." His tone, filled with genuine concern, but laced with excitement at the prospect of seeing her at the old farmhouse.

Ten minutes away, Matt's butterflies gave him the nervous giggles, and he tried Eva again. "Hey, you. I'm ten minutes from the house. Can't wait to see you. Love you."

* * * * *

As Matthias approached the final mile of his journey, he had his annoyed and agitated feeling. And worry. Worry he'd still not heard from Eva. He didn't like not hearing from her at the best of times. But especially today.

He turned into the old farmhouse entrance; he didn't see the SALE AGREED sign. What he saw turned his blood cold. Bile rose in his throat. His heart rate increasing and thumping loud in his ears. He felt sick. Nauseous.

There in front of the house was the abandoned getaway car. The three remaining doors were wide open. The fourth door was missing. The rear windscreen was shattered. The front door to farmhouse wide open too. Not good.

And lying on the gravel, a bloodied purple balaclava.

A sign of the impending collision of his world and Jude's.

24:10

"Get her out of here!" Jude had barked, his authoritative command cutting through the chaos.

Gerasim and Draško had already jumped into the car, deciding to leave Eva where she lay.

"Now!" Jude screamed at them.

Jumping out of the car, adrenaline coursing through their veins, they bundled the wounded Eva into the getaway car. Draško took opportunity to drop his 'baseball bat' under the car. *Fuck it, it is not traceable.*

The quiet pavement and road had suddenly got all crowded and bunched up with onlookers and stopped cars as Gerasim smoked the rear wheels of the black getaway car, leaving burnt black rubber on the tarmac, and the car's rear door under the wheels of the bus, as they screeched off, bumping the curb to clear the bus, then dropping back onto a clear road.

Eva was laid across the back seat, her head on her father's lap. Her legs and pelvis crushed and broken, white bone poking through the ripped overalls, contrasting with the black material. Blood oozed through the mouth and nose holes in her purple balaclava.

"Fuck!" screamed Draško from the front passenger seat. Holding his head in his hands, bouncing his knees up and down. If he'd ever needed the toilet, it was now.

Gerasim was silent. Yes, he was focused on keeping the car at a good speed and clear of traffic. But he was now convinced allowing a woman to be part of the job had brought the bad luck. *And now this was the baddest of luck*, he thought, as he caught sight of his boss in the rear-view mirror.

Jude was feeling sick. He'd promised there'd be no guns. Had his gun gone off and hit his daughter? *No, it wasn't my fault. It was the plebby staff member. If he hadn't tried to be a hero, I wouldn't have had to use the gun.*

He was holding Eva tight across her midriff, making sure she didn't move around too much, or slide out of the car altogether, as Gez took bend after bend at speed. Jude had always been a strong figure, taking charge, making decisions, barking commands, but with his daughter lying here dying - he knew she was - thoughts and words and actions were failing him. His primary motivation had always been how to steer clear of prison, stay free. *How the fuck was that going to happen now? What the fuck am I going to do? Why the fuck wasn't she already in the car? Stupid girl. The gun's not traceable.*

A mile or so into the countryside, Jude ditched the gun out of the void where the car's rear door used to be.

Eva was almost catapulted into the rear footwell as Gez braked and screeched into the turning for the old farmhouse, just missing Renborough Brothers' SALE AGREED sign, and careened to a panicked stop in front of the weathered structure. Jude tightened his grip to prevent her falling, but the swerve and sudden halt sent his head slamming against the window and then forward into the seat in front, breaking a lens in his glasses.

Jude had been happy to help buy the house. Not simply for his daughter, but more for his own self interests. It stood isolated and silent, away from prying eyes. A great getaway stopover after a job. A sanctuary. He did not imagine his first use of the house would be like this; *Not much of a fuckin' sanctuary right now*, the thought running through his head as he stepped out of the car into a chilly afternoon. Whether it was Eva's horrendous wounds, the bang to his nose, or the hot rubber and smoking brakes, but to Jude, the air was acrid. He couldn't breathe. *Stupid, stupid girl.*

* * * * *

As he sped along in Eva's little yellow car, Matt's anxiousness grew with every passing mile, with every minute his phone didn't ring or ping. The autumn afternoon sun cast long shadows across the road, eerily shaped shadow after eerily shaped shadow flickered light and dark across his field of vision.

He dialled Eva's number.

* * * * *

Brains rattled, adrenaline still rushing through his body, pain in his face, and his authoritative demeanour eclipsed by worry, but mostly with concern for his own self-preservation, Jude didn't hear the ringing phone. Nor did his two goons.

Jude took the balaclava off, discarded it on the gravel, and gave orders to bring Eva inside. "Gently! Carefully!", he barked as Gez and Dizzy, shaking with fear and worry, rushed to open the car door. Everything was a blur as Jude thrust open the farmhouse front door, allowing Eva's fragile body to make its journey from the car to the old sofa. Her body and face, once full of vitality and beauty, now lay limp, crushed and bloodied.

Inside, the atmosphere was a suffocating mix of misery and panic and disbelief. Draško dashed upstairs to find the toilet. Gerasim placed a consoling hand on Jude's shoulder before retiring to the kitchen to get some water. Jude stayed in the living room, watching over Eva, literally watching her life ebb away, helpless. Bloodstains and rips and tears marred Eva's overalls, a visceral reminder of the brutality they couldn't escape.

* * * * *

Ten minutes away, Matt's butterflies gave him the nervous giggles, and he tried Eva again. "Hey, you. I'm ten minutes from the house. Can't wait to see you. Love you."

* * * * *

Kneeling next to Eva, Jude heard now her phone ringing. *Shit! Matty.* He'd completely forgotten about Matty. He reached into her overall pocket and pulled the phone out.

Three missed calls.

Two voicemails.

One boyfriend. Jude refused to use the correct, common 'f' term.

Despite his ability to be a straight-up cold-feeling bastard, Jude could not bring himself to put the phone to Eva's face to get access. Besides, it was unlikely the phone would recognise her features covered in that much blood. And fingerprint access? Somehow, it seemed more inappropriate. *If I could access the phone, I could buy some time, I could -*

Eva jolted, coughed up blood, and took rasping, laboured breaths. It wasn't a sign of a miracle recovery. Nor was it a sign of consciousness. Just her body's transition to the shallow respirations, the terminal restlessness. The body working at the process of dying.

Jude dropped the phone and reached out to hold his daughter's mottled, blotchy hand, trying to comfort her.

Or comfort himself.

* * * * *

Car tyres crunched out the front.

A car door slammed.

Jude joined Gez in the kitchen, knowing that they were about to face a storm and there'd surely be safety in numbers. Three against one to front-up to Matty about what had happened. To calm him down. Talk him through his loss. Offer support.

Or protect each other, should the need arise. Find a way out of this mess.

There was nothing that could be done, nothing to be done. The harsh reality of what had happened, what was happening, would irreversibly alter everything.

Forever.

25:9

Her father had said they'd be in and out in less than four minutes.

Four minutes became another four minutes. And that was six minutes ago.

Ten minutes behind schedule.

Eva's heart was racing. She was guarding the Post Office's main entrance. One foot in the overheated premises, one foot out on the pavement, in the chilly autumn air. Her role was twofold: first, to prevent any incoming members of the public, which was going okay - the pedestrian footfall was thankfully quiet. Second, to ensure a smooth path to the waiting black getaway car, in which Gerasim was waiting.

Gerasim had been as grim as his nickname. Yes, he'd been questioning and moaning about the timings, the route there, the escape route out, and the whole plan all morning. *For fuck's sake*, he'd been involved in all the planning from the beginning. But his disgust and hatred of Eva, of women, was the grim she was implying. She'd heard him say to Draško that the 'stupid bitch' would bring bad luck to the job, so it was a good thing that she was only having to stand by the door. And it was a good job he wasn't allowed to have a gun.

She had decided not to react, and just pretended she hadn't heard. She'd thought about walking away, but decided she could deal with it because of the money. She acknowledged that her decision was, in itself, pretty grim. *Grim.* She thought of Matt. Loved that he called Gez Grim. She couldn't wait to see Matt soon. Be with him, celebrate this, her last job, and celebrate their new 'old' farmhouse.

* * * * *

It was coming up to quarter-past-three in the afternoon, and Matthias was feeling his annoyed and agitated feeling. And worried. Worry he'd not heard from Eva. She had said the job would be done by three and, despite the no phones rule, she'd drop him a text as soon as they were away and heading over to the farmhouse.

Bollocks to it! He picked up his phone...

* * * * *

Eva wanted to shout to her father, to find out what the problem was. But looking like a cliché criminal - overalls and purple balaclava – was bad enough, but if she called out, witnesses would know she was a woman.

A woman in a purple balaclava, they'd say. Surely, she would be easier to track down with that description.

Draško was holding the main floor, keeping everyone on the ground with their heads down. He wasn't doing too bad a job, seeing as all he had was a baseball bat wrapped in a black bin bag. The closest thing any of them had resembling a gun. He was bouncing and fidgeting like a nervous schoolkid who needed the toilet. Actually, him being Dung, he probably did.

She tried to catch her father's eye and convey her concern about the time elapsed so far. Looked beyond the wriggling Dung, she saw her father packing cash into the holdalls. 'Grab the cash delivery before it hits the books and gets put in the safe,' Jude, her father, had said. 'Four minutes tops'. But he was still rifling money into the bags. *C'mon, Dad. Hurry up!* she thought.

Draško didn't like the way Eva was flitting her head in his direction. It made him nervous. Made him need the toilet, desperately. Ger was right, she was bringing bad luck. He knew they were running late. *She's probably casting a spell on me to shit myself right here. If she doesn't stop now, I will run unwrap this Pigeon 1 Sporter and -*

A shout, a crash, and a holler from behind the counter. Eva and Draško saw Jude struggling with an overzealous member of staff. A small kerfuffle. But then, in a matter of seconds, he'd thrown the employee off and was out from behind the counter and heading onto the floor toward Draško, waving to the door.

The Post Office had an old ringing alarm, its siren now blaring. Well, at least they knew when the alarm had triggered, so no sneaky coppers turning up unannounced despite the overrunning schedule.

Trouble was, with the alarm now shrieking, a small crowd started gathering.

Shitting hell! Her heart rate must be topping a hundred-and-fifty plus, sweat trickling down inside her balaclava. *Here we go!* She was glad this was her last job. *Oh Matt, I am so with you after this. Just me and you. I wish we'd never agreed to this. I am sorry. Give me a minute more and -*

Dad is out from behind the counter. Check. He's closing in on Dung. Check. They're exiting the Post Office faster than the Horizon system cleared out the sub-postmasters. Check.

Eva stepped out onto the pavement. Despite the public gathering, the path to the getaway car remained clear. Check. She darted to the getaway car.

"Open the doors, you stupid witch!" Dung screamed at her, as he turned back to see where his boss was.

She yanked opened the nearside passenger doors. Check.

Dung then Dad stepped onto the pavement. Check.

She darted round to the driver's side of the car, grabbed the rear door handle, pulled the door open. Check.

* * * * *

Matt called Eva's phone. Let it ring a few times.

* * * * *

Her phone rang. Check.

No, not check!

What the fuck!?

Her mind went blank for a second. She paused by the open door, confused. The shrill of her phone continued. *It should be on silent. I've got gloves on. It's still ringing.* Muscle memory, automatic response kicked in and she fumbled in her overalls for her phone. She doesn't reach it.

Bang! Bang!

Gunshots!

That's not a check, either.

Eva looked over the top of the car and saw her father running toward the getaway car but pointing a gun back into the Post Office. She then sees him bring the gun back round, but he's lost his balance, he's stumbled, stumbled, bumped into Draško, knocking him off balance too, loosening his grip on the wrapped baseball bat -

Bang!

The car's rear window shatters.

Her left leg gives way beneath her.

The searing pain -

Wham!

The bus hits Eva.

She bounces off the car door's edge with enough force to take both her and the car door out into the road and crashing onto the tarmac. Stunned, her hand still stuck in her overall pocket, she's unable to move out of the way of the rear wheel of the bus.

26:8

The ringtone stopped. A beep. A click.

The fucking answer machine kicks in and does its thing: churning out the pre-recorded gruff, husky Spanish voice, travelling electrically, converting to a sound wave, coming through to Matthias's phone and into his ear, as he listened to the short, quiet hum of the answer machine as it delivered her message.

"Hola, soy Alma. Gracias por llamar. Por favor, deja tu nombre, tu número y un breve mensaje, y me pondré en contacto contigo tan pronto como sea posible. Gracias."

Alma's voice really grated on him. Maybe it was because she managed to mis-navigate the natural ebb and flow and inflections and accentuation of her own mother tongue in a way that disrupted the rhythm of the one of the world's most beautiful, romantic languages. Maybe it was the nasal undertones beneath the croak of her voice. Maybe it was because she had the habit of always following up with poor English.

"Hello, is Alma. Please leave a message and I call you in the next time."

Or maybe it was because Alma garnered more of Eva's attention and time these days than he did. Or so it felt.

Another click and beep and pause, then, "Alma, it's Matthias. I'm looking for Eva... if you're there, please pick up."

He paced a few steps from one side of the living room - about four small strides in the small suburban house - waiting to see if Alma answered. He felt a little self-conscious making the call; a tad embarrassed and ashamed to be chasing to find out where Eva was. But not as ashamed as he was agitated. Eva had said she'd be out for a couple of hours and wasn't back yet. Ashamed. Agitated. But neither of those as much as he was worried.

Matt wandered back through to the small dining room and sat in front of his laptop, as the deafening silence played in his ear. "Okay, you're not there -"

He clicked into Alma's social media page, greeted by her profile picture, which focused in on her big dark eyes staring out into the ether. Her angular face framed by her long black hair.

A scroll down to the most recent post on Alma's social media page, and Matthias read:

@EvaM96 is come see me today. Luv my hermosa chica, la reina XOXOX

"So, it's just...it's...I'm, er, looking for Eva... I said that already... I wondered if she was still with you?" Matthias asked the answer machine. "She said she was going to see you for a reading, and, well, she said she'd only be a couple of hours and I expected her back by now," he added.

Matt switched his laptop screen over to Eva's social media site. Her shoulder length hair, her blue eyes, her soft lips; it was a gorgeous photo. Matt had convinced her to use it as her profile picture. The bit that aggravated him was that she'd set her profile image over a background picture of Jude, Grim and Dung, each image tagged with their names. The three of them giving a 'Hear No, See No, Speak No' pose. *Monkeys? Apes more like. Jude, Grim and Dung. Far from wise. Wankers!* he thought. It was like they were goading him.

"But you're not there, so you can't tell me." Matthias continued his one-sided conversation with Alma's answer machine. He clicked the laptop's mouse pad and tracked the curser down to Eva's social media posts, reading a comment addressed to Alma:

Got another session with @AlmaS, my #Spanish psíquica. See you soon xxx

Posted several hours earlier.

"I guess she might've called in to see her father," he muttered, hovering the curser over the image of Jude. Matt places two fingers on the screen, spread them apart, enlarging the image, so that Jude was front and centre. At well over six-foot and built like the proverbial shithouse, he didn't take that much screen expansion. "But I'm not calling Jude," Matthias mumbled to himself.

Switching a laptop window back to Alma's site, he continued, "Anyway, I'm rambling. If you see her, get her to call me, yeah, and let me know where she is... that she's okay."

Matt scrolled down Alma's social page. "Maybe she thinks we've already moved to the new house... the old house," he chuckles to himself, at his poor humour. "Look, just get her to let me know what time she'll be home," he adds.

He clicks on the most recent video file. The thumbnail shows Alma standing by an old, empty leather armchair, in front of shelves of knick-knacks. Pressing play, on the screen, Alma presents her left hand, its ink-striped fingers; index and middle digits - *two, four... six, eight* - before using it to direct the viewer to look at the chair, like a magician asks an audience to watch the top hat before the rabbit appears. The video is just a few seconds long and nothing else happens.

"Anyway, thanks... bye". Matt ends the call, placing the phone next to a silver cigarette case.

A new post pops up on Alma's timeline.

Great session with @EvaM96

A love heart emoji pops up in response. From Eva.

Matthias opens the silver case and runs his fingers over the two cigarettes contained within.

A ping and a flicker on the screen caught Matt's eye, and a second video file appeared and started auto-playing. It shows Alma standing silently in front of the still empty but now half-burnt, smouldering armchair. She stares coldly into the camera, then turns it away from herself and focuses it on the chair, bringing it closer and closer to the screen, the charred and burnt leather becoming more prevalent.

Matt slams shut his laptop, bringing his searches to a close.

27:7

Jude stomped into the dining room.

He thought about storming out of the house altogether, but he didn't want to give Matty the satisfaction. He'd stay a little longer. He could play awkwardly, too. "Right, are we fuckin' sorted? We don't fuck this up! Anyone got anything to add?"

"It's my last job." Eva spoke up. She'd promised Matt she'd force the point home this evening.

"Yes, it's your last job. Alright!?" Jude raised his eyebrows at his daughter, hitting home his frustration and bitterness at her decision, not to mention her repetition of the counter-conditions she and Matty had come back at him with. "It's all we've heard. Enough!"

Eva felt the heat in her face as it got a little flushed. She didn't like her father's temper rising.

"We've been through the whole fucking thing. Now, we stick to it, and we're sorted. We're not tooled up for this… No guns. No phones. No trouble. Done. Clean. Back to the old farmhouse for afternoon tea." Jude turned to Matthias. "Happy!?" he sneered. "Now, shall we have the man of the house bring us some coffee?" he instructed, rather than asked, bringing a firm close to the planning session.

Christ, Matt really riled Dad outside, thought Eva.

Gerasim and Draško roll up the maps as Matthias brought fresh coffee through to the living room, where the evening was to conclude.

Jude had parked himself in Matt's armchair again. Gerasim and Draško had planted themselves on the sofa, sitting on the blanket. Again. So, Matthias and Eva were leaning against the fireplace, above which the 'I LOVE YOU EVA' Post-its still proudly showed their colours.

Everyone sipped their coffee. Silence. No one would look at any of the others. You could cut the atmosphere with a knife, to quote a cliché.

Awkward.

Matthias was smiling inside.

Draško was fidgeting on the sofa, bouncing his legs like a child - *maybe Dung needs the fucking toilet again*, Matt smirked – as Gerasim gave Draško a little elbow nudge of encouragement.

"So that some of your writing, Matty?" Draško piped up, pointing to the Post-its.

Gurning like the fucking Dung he is, thought Matt.

Gerasim joined in, "Eva says you have book published. Do we get a friends copy? My woman likes to read. She reads Heat magazine," he ridiculed his girlfriend to the group, "But I am sure she would make effort for a free book, so long as it is an easy read, like the love notes on the wall, eh? I don't want to make it hard on her little woman brain," he added, aiming the jibe at Matthias.

Matt said nothing.

Eva put her lips to Matt's ear and whispered something to him. He gave a little nod and made his way out of the room, only pausing swiftly, smoothly, but a tad aggressively, to yank the purple blanket from under Dung's arse and hand it to Eva. "Hope it doesn't smell too bad," he chuckled and left the room.

Draško's nostrils flared as he gritted his teeth in anger. He glanced to his right and saw Gerasim make a gun shape with his fingers. The two Slavs nodded their understanding.

Eva scrunched her blanket up and held it against her midriff. She didn't see Grim and Dung's mimed threat to Matt.

"Was that while you two concocted your plan to make this an arduous and laborious evening?" Jude jutted his chin toward the Post-its, raising his voice a little as he ended the question. "I can use big words too, Matty!" he shouted toward the kitchen.

"Don't, Dad, okay?" Eva pleaded quietly to her father.

Gerasim and Draško sat more upright, reacting to the bit of backchat and tension. A daughter should not speak to her father like that; she'd been bolshy all evening. The two of them weren't impressed that a woman was to be part of the job. It was no place for a woman. They only cause trouble. And here she was, causing trouble… and trouble for her father, no less. And they didn't like it when Jude was in a bad mood.

"You've bleated on about it being your last job… no guns. He's fucking wimping about making coffee and going on about quitting smoking… writing fuckin' love notes. He's been creating an awkward atmosphere all evening. Even outside, he was fucking difficult. I go out there to be pleasant and… and… he riles me -"

Jude bit his tongue as Matthias returned to the front room, joining Eva by the fireplace. The two of them hold hands. Matthias takes something out of his pocket.

"We've got something to tell you," says Eva, shakily.

Matthias places the ring on Eva's left-hand ring finger, holding her close to him supportively.

"We're getting married." Eva smiles at her father. "Dad?"

Perhaps he has got some fucking balls, thought Jude. He held his daughter's pleading stare for a few uncomfortable seconds, then held his arms out welcomely, *Hey, I've got to do my fatherly duty, I suppose,* but more with reluctance. He needed the fourth man for the job, and Eva was it. It was too late to find a bloke for the job at this late stage. Besides, she now owed him. And he needed this job to be a success.

Eva went in for a hug. Perhaps her father was becoming just that, a father?

Matthias smiled smugly at Jude, sure that Jude hated him even more in that moment. Matt having ignored their conversation in the garden. And he sees Grim and Dung smiling and relaxing back into the sofa. Maybe they're convinced that the joyful nuptial news has eased the tension.

Eva stepped back to join Matt again.

Matt held Jude's stare for a second, then held the gaze of Grim and Dung. Then he repeated the eye contact with all three of them.

Now let's finish the evening with awkward, he thought.

"If anything happens to Eva, I will kill you."

28:6

As he traversed from the dining room through the kitchen towards the back door, Jude caught sight of the gun on the kitchen worktop and paused for a second before stepping outside. The temperature in the back garden had the expected but pleasant autumn evening chill.

Matthias didn't just hear the clink of his Zippo opening. he embraced it. Then he relished the roll of his thumb over the flint to get the beautiful rough rasp that led to the flame. He lit the tobacco and then took a deep drag on the cigarette with welcomed pleasure, then shut the lighter with the reliable clunk. He exhaled a cloud of smoke into the cold evening air, his warm breath mixed with the cigarette smoke and clouded his view of the ascending moon. Mesmerising. He'd miss smoking.

He watched his smoke rise into the evening air, only for it to be followed up by a thicker cloud of pungent smoke.

Cigar smoke.

Jude stepped into Matt's peripheral vision, and the air turned a little colder. "Matty."

Matthias, with nothing he wanted to say to Jude, not wanting to talk to him, gave a small, slight nod of his head and took another drag on his cigarette.

"Eva's on board," Jude said with an air of smugness through another cloud of cigar smoke.

Matthias took a sidestep away. He really didn't want to engage in conversation at all. But He and Eva so wanted the old farmhouse. Needed it. They'd pinned their hopes, dreams and forever happiness to it. He owed it to Eva, not to himself or Jude. But he wanted to be awkward. "What else did you expect? You put the condition on it."

"I offered, Matty. Mind what you fucking say, yeah!? I offered to help. Eva took it up. She's a good girl, my Evie. Keeps to her word. Loves her dad," Jude added, clearly poking to get a rise out of Matthias. "Family's important."

For a moment, Matt couldn't believe the audacity of the man. *You are fuckin' joking me?*

"That why you let her mother walk out? Let Eva carry the guilt... the loss? Why you packed her off to boarding school as soon as you could, huh? So much quality time... right?" Matthias questioned, not expecting a response. He knew nothing more than what Eva had told him over their time together, what she'd said at the lakes, but he knew she never lied. The same could not be said about Jude. People like him, nothing's their fault. It's always someone else who's wrong. Maybe he shouldn't have said anything, shouldn't have made this little dig at Jude, but he'd vowed to play awkward.

* * * * *

Jude was glad when his wife had stormed out. One less burden in his life. She'd had the 'Big C' but it was him who was sick - sick of having to look after her, take her to appointments, pick up her medication, run Eva here, there, and everywhere. Sticking the piece on the kitchen worktop was the straw that broke the camel's back. He knew it would.

She'd not taken Eva with her when she left. He tracked her down to some refuge hostel and told her she had to take her daughter. 'I haven't got the strength', she'd whined. As far as Jude was concerned, the lazy cow was being selfish, not taking her responsibilities for the child seriously; the responsibility that society expected of a woman, a mother. It was not his fucking job to look after the girl. Making time and breakfast and lunch and dinner for Eva, shouting at her to put her toys away, bellowing at her to stop crying, had been a long, aggravating two-year-long chore, right up to the point he was able to send her off to boarding school. The fuckers didn't take them until they were seven. And it cost him a fucking fortune. Only then did he get some of the freedom he craved, needed. His life and time were far too important for any female to be part of. He was thankful he could palm Eva off on babysitters and the TV, when she came home now and then. And, as weak as he thought Matty was, he couldn't believe his luck when she wanted to move in with him. But he'd never tell Eva or Matty any of that.

* * * * *

Jude said nothing.

Definitely awkward.

They say it takes seven minutes to smoke a cigarette. Matt could burn one down in four, maybe three, on a quick fag break. He took two really quick, deep drags on the tobacco, trying to bring this encounter to a swift conclusion.

A slight adjustment in posture, a subtle change in body language, and Jude looked to take control. "I got no problem helping out with the money, Matty. My girl wants the house. What else was I gonna do? I know my duty as a father. I needed a fourth person for the job. Birmingham Eddie couldn't make it, so it made sense to keep it in the family. Sets us up with a nice payday. Money. It's what you want, huh?"

Matt said nothing. He took two more deep draws on his cigarette.

"You rushing that smoke, Matty?"

Matt inhaled and then exhaled a long plume of smoke. "I've promised Eva I'll quit. My last smokes, her last job."

"Wimping again. Man-up, Matty. My daughter shouldn't be the breadwinner. She's a woman. She should be in the home, cooking, having kids." Jude prodded, trying to keep the upper hand.

"Can you hear yourself? Drag yourself out of the last century, Jude. Women work. But I don't want Eva working with you, working for you, working with Grim and Dung -"

Jude raised an eyebrow and a tiny smirk, quietly impressed with Matt's dig at his boys, but not wanting to show it. "They're good lads. They've been loyal to me since the day I found 'em, when they were young and wet behind the ears. I stood up in court and gave them a good, solid character reference. Do you think I'd do that for someone who didn't deserve it, eh!?"

"You giving a good character reference? There's a fucking oxymoron!"

"Ooh, oxymoron. Big word. That a writer's word, Matty... you're a writer, right?" Jude aimed a dig back at Matthias.

"What's that supposed to mean?"

"Oh, nothin'... stickers on the wall, fuckin' love notes...I dunno! Stop being so sensitive, Matty. Stop being soft. Man the fuck up, boy!"

"Like those two cunts in there!? Like -" Matt stopped himself from adding Jude to the list and finished his spat in his head. *Like you, you selfish bastard?* "I've got a publishing contract. Money will be coming in soon, so we won't need you. And me and Eva are getting married. That man enough for you?"

The comment hit Jude harder than he wanted, than he expected. He needed to up his game. "I know. I saw her hand at the house the other day. Not a fuckin' word to me from you, or

Eva. You trying to make up for it now, eh!? Is this you asking me for my daughter's hand? Get fucked!"

"I wouldn't ask you for anything, Jude. Eva's everything to me. I love her. I really fuckin' love her. We've agreed to your deal, your condition, but then we're out of it. We get to be together on our terms."

"You think this deal means we're done? You've got another think coming, boy!"

Matthias didn't like the way this was going. He tossed his cigarette. "I'm going to make more coffee," he said, as he turned to go back into the house.

"Mind that gun on the kitchen worktop, Matty. If you ever have kids... Eva's mother would turn in her grave."

29:5

Matthias wasn't being unhelpful.

He always pulled his weight with the household chores. Happy to do his share of the cleaning, tidying, cooking, washing-up. But today he was hovering in the kitchen, slowly brewing coffee, watching and listening to Eva flitting and faffing and beavering around.

He wasn't being unhelpful.

He was deliberately being awkward.

Instead of writing upstairs in the small bedroom-cum-office, as he usually did, today he'd brought pretty much everything downstairs and put it all over the dining room table. His laptop, his whiteboard, his Post-its, his A4 pads, his pens, a couple of manuscripts, all spread across the table. Despite his promise to Eva to quit smoking, he'd even brought his smoking paraphernalia down. His Zippo lighter was resting on his cigarette case. It still contained his last three cigarettes. He'd admired his own willpower so far, but if he was going to break his promise, it'd be today.

Yes, he was being awkward. And there were two reasons.

Firstly, a reticent one. Eva had announced she was going to see her spiritualist, Alma, next week. Again. Matthias didn't like Alma, but Eva said she had a lot to talk about, so he had agreed. Of course, Eva didn't need his permission, but he knew she sought his acquiescence.

Secondly, a repugnant one. Jude and his two Eastern European goons were coming over for a planning meeting;

planning the deal, the condition that Jude had put to them. Put to them? That sounded like it was optional, but it wasn't. Well, it was, because there's always a choice. But a choice to stay in this part of town and fumble through life was not a choice if Matt and Eva wanted out and wanted to follow their destiny, their dream. Matthias would not make it easy for Jude to steamroll through the house and their lives like a bull in a china shop, like he usually did.

Matthias was determined to make it awkward for Jude.

* * * * *

Eva knew why Matt had put his stuff all over the dining room table. And she knew he hadn't written a word all day long. She'd seen him scribble on a few Post-its, but not much else. She would not call him out about it; would not moan or dig at him for not helping clear the table. Not today.

She gathered his stuff into a neat pile - small notes, A4 pads, manuscripts stacked on the laptop - then placed them into the corner of the room. "How's it going? It makes me happy to see you writing." She said, guiltily. She knew she had nothing to be guilty about, but she somehow felt it.

"Yeah, it's going okay," Matt replied, entering the dining room. He picked up his pile of stuff and placed it back on the table and started thumbing through the Post-its.

"Matt," Eva sighed, pleading politely, determined not to whine, "I need the table -"

Matthias grabbed her hand. "Wanna see something I've written today?" he asked, leading her into the small living room. "Sit. Sit."

Eva popped herself on the corner of the sofa, her left hand reaching out to clutch a clump of her purple blanket and watched as Matt started sticking the Post-its on the wall above the small fireplace. "What is it with you and Post-its, eh!?" she laughed.

Matthias took a step back to reveal his work. On the wall, the Post-its read:

I LOVE YOU EVA.

Eva pulled her blanket into her bosom and cackled with laughter. "And?" she asked.

Matt smiled, stepped over to the sofa, and kissed her. "Yes... and And".

Eva slipped off her engagement ring and handed it to him. Matt popped it in his jeans pocket and asked if she wanted coffee. To which she nodded.

Matthias returned to the kitchen, to the coffee. Eva stopped in the dining room to clear the dining room table. Again.

* * * * *

A knock at the front door.

Matthias took the ring out of his pocket and reached up to the top kitchen cupboard. He removed the gun, placed it on the kitchen worktop near the kettle, took out some mugs. He put the ring in the cupboard just as he heard the knock at the front door. He paused, simply holding the cupboard handle, but stared at the empty mugs. He hoped it wasn't Jude. He knew it was him, but he hoped it wasn't. Then he heard Jude's voice greeting Eva. Distracted, Matt grimaced, shook his head, and shut the cupboard door. He was surprised that Jude even bothered to knock; figuring he'd have a key or just kick it down. "Coffee?" he shouted, with no welcoming inflection.

"Nice to see you too, Matty," shouted Jude in a monotone drawl, his mocking sarcasm obvious. "And get some for Gez and Dizzy. They'll be here in a minute. They're just trying to park. It's fuckin' tight on your road, ain't it?"

Matt rolled his eyes. *Sarcastic cunt*, he thought, before hearing the front door close, followed by the mumbled greetings of Gerasim and Draško arriving. Gez and Dizzy, Jude called them, because he was lazy. Matt nicknamed them Grim and Dung, because he was a little more creative. He didn't think the nicknames fit at first; Grim and Dung painted the picture of likeable, funny hobbits. It didn't really suit two burly six-foot Slavs. But he stuck with it, kept slipping into using the alternative names. He decided the dichotomy felt right. He didn't call them that to their faces, of course.

"What is the fuckin' fuck, Matty!?" Gerasim loudly shouted, his deep, gruff Slavic intonation placing emphasis on the consonants.

"You are romantic, soppy bastard, Matty!" Draško added, with a softer pitch, and a volume turned down from a ten to an eight, when compared to his slightly shorter, smaller framed but just as tall friend.

Grim and Dung have seen the Post-its, Matt realised. *The only love they'd ever had was probably their time in prison, bending over for the soap in the showers, no doubt.*

Gerasim and Draško sniggered like schoolboys at their own mickey-taking; the two muttering and chuckling to one another. Well, not chuckling, so much as guffawing. It wasn't exactly subtle.

A thorny silence trailed Matthias as he brought the tray of coffees into the now crowded living room.

It was small enough when it was just the two of them, but adding the unwelcome guests Jude, Grim and Dung – each of them over six-feet tall - it felt claustrophobic; positively rammed. Jude had planted himself in Matt's armchair, and Grim and Dung had plonked themselves on the sofa, making it look even smaller than it was. They'd not even moved Eva's blanket, which was now wedged under Dung's arse.

Eva had had to squat on the floor by the fireplace. This annoyed Matt.

Pissed off, Matthias handed out the coffees without saying a word before heading back to the kitchen.

He'd made sure their guests had a drink.

Not unhelpful.

But he didn't have to make small talk.

Awkward.

* * * * *

On the living room floor, there were street maps of Renborough and the three smaller nearby towns and their suburbs. Crosses and dots and routes, marked out with red pen, highlighted key areas on the maps. Jude and Gerasim were pawing over the indicated areas, as Eva nodded in understanding.

"Should we be worried about Dung, Grim?" asked Eva. "Sorry, I mean Dizzy, Gez." Hoping she'd corrected herself quickly enough and Grim hadn't picked up on the 'accidentally on purpose' slip of the tongue.

The toilet flushed.

Had she called Dizzy 'dung', or was that just said because it was the second time he'd gone to answer the call of nature? Gerasim had heard and understood Eva just fine. But she was Jude's daughter – it was her only saving grace stopping Gerasim bringing her down a peg or two, putting her in a woman's rightful place. And he'd been on the end of Jude's temper twice before and it wasn't something he wanted repeated.

"Dras, he is okay. New surroundings... nervous... he got to take a shit. He used to stink the jail cell out, I tell you. If I had not been so understanding, I would have been on my own, in solitary for the whole of my sentence." Gerasim explained.

Gerasim, being a couple of years older, felt protective of Draško. They'd known each other since childhood. They'd survived then fled the Yugoslav troubles at the back end of the nineties and made the long, arduous journey to the eastern shores of England. The two of them were trying to steal a van, which turned out to be Jude's van. Since that first arrival in the UK twenty years ago, both had worked for Jude's building company as general labourers, but mostly getting their hands criminally dirty, when Jude needed them to.

Surprisingly, their recent time behind bars wasn't because of one of Jude's jobs. It was a GBH charge. They should've served the full three years they got from the judge, but they'd worked together to be model prisoners and get an early release on good behaviour. Gerasim's girlfriend didn't want to press any charges against either of them. That had helped. And if the police weren't parked outside the supermarket that day - seeing Ger hit her, and then seeing Dras throw her to the floor when she'd lashed out, then kick her when she was down - there would have been no case against them. The cowardly shoppers would never have said a word.

Jude had played the whole incident down, not wanting the 'anti-misogyny, women's lib' earache from Eva. He kept their jobs open for when they got out.

Draško came back to the living room. "Irritable belly wassname. IBS," he exclaimed, putting his hands up in a mock surrender. "I would not go there for a while. Might add flavour to the coffee."

Gerasim laughed.

Eva didn't find toilet humour humorous, "Dizzy dung guts, eh?" but she enjoyed aiming the subtle dig at Draško. She never liked the fact that in their house, like a lot of old terraced houses, you had to go through the kitchen to get to the bathroom. She heard Matt coughing in the kitchen. Now she hated the fact.

Gerasim and Draško. Grim and Dung. Aptly nicknamed by Matt.

Draško wasn't quick to pick up on Eva's ridicule aimed at him. His high cheekbones and dark brown eyes screwed up with a confused look that distorted his pug-like face. He ran both his hands through his buzz-cut hair, and figured that if Gerasim was laughing, then he must have made a good joke. Gerasim wouldn't allow girls to make fun of him.

Jude rolled up the maps and strode into the small dining room, where he unrolled them on the table. The others followed him in.

Matthias stepped into the dining room doorway, cigarette case and Zippo in hand. He flipped open the cigarette case and shows Eva that there's still three cigarettes in there. "I'm just going to step out back for a smoke. Then I'll make some more coffee."

Eva nodded and smiled at Matt, understanding his need for respite.

Jude took a cigar from his top pocket, rolled it around, licked his lips, and popped the cigar between his teeth. "Think I'll join Matty." he announced, smirking at his daughter, and nodded for her and Gez and Dizzy to go over the plans once again.

"Be nice." Eva said to her father.

30:4

The walls of the pedestrian underpass under the main A-road out of Renborough were a colourful montage of council-sponsored art and random graffiti, illuminated by the strip lighting.

Matthias liked this route home from the lakes. It was their usual route. He liked the underpass's choice of directions from which to exit. Liked the colours and words on the walls. Liked the echo of their footsteps providing a rhythmic beat to the hum of the road above. Liked that their exit took them via the bottom end of Silver Street, the area of town where he'd spent much of his youth.

And he liked it even more this evening because Eva had won Poohsticks again, so the dare was hers to do. Again. Not a dare as bold as the last time she'd won, but she couldn't do that here, not with the risk of the public entering the underpass. But a quick flash of her breasts was good enough for him. Matthias could never understand why she insisted on the winner doing a dare. *Who does that? Surely a dare is a forfeit, not a prize?* Eva never ceased to amaze him.

The evening light fading, Matthias and Eva descend into the harsh fluorescent lights of the underpass, casting an urban pallor on their surroundings; a contrast to the idyllic lake walk they'd left behind.

They'd discussed the condition that her father had put to them - he'd stump up the money they needed, but on the proviso that Eva took the job offer. They'd weighed it up.

They'd told him she would, but straight out, bottom line, that was it. It would be the last time. And they told him they had their own conditions...

But they'd told him nothing else.

The echo of their footsteps became a little louder as they walked deeper through the underpass, the two of them holding hands. In just a few more steps, Matthias noticed a shadow against the wall on the turn ahead. It was looming larger, moving closer, and the echo of the shadow owner's footsteps soon joined their own. Rarely did they see anyone else when they came home this way. Matthias squeezed Eva's hand a little tighter as the shadow detached itself from the darkness, and a figure emerged, strobing under the flickering strip lights, making its moves look like it a badly pixelated video game character. Its face obscured by a purple balaclava. Wielding a gun. Ominous.

The sight of the black and silver steel in the mugger's hand sent a shiver through Eva; a nausea that wrenched her stomach. Images of her mum leaving, her father clearing items from a kitchen worktop, the condition she and Matt had put to her father. Her chest burnt when she gasped.

Matt heard Eva's sharp intake of breath and felt her lean in closer to him. He felt his heartbeat quicken as the fight-or-flight adrenaline fluttered in his stomach. The inevitable face-to-balaclava standoff happened at the corner of the Silver Street exit. The exit they needed to take. The exit ramp would be just fifty yards up to the safety of the busy A-road.

But Balaclava stood in their way. The stark reality of danger sent a chill through the air.

"Phones, money, jewellery. Now!" Balaclava's demand echoed against the cold, colourful tiles. The barrel of the gun glinted intermittently and malevolently beneath the blinking strip light, as the hooded stranger pointed it at Eva.

Matthias didn't give a fuck about the phones and the little cash they had, *But this cunt wasn't hurting Eva.* If Matt had been on his own, he would have resigned himself to handing over stuff. Reluctantly, yes, but he would have done it just to avoid trouble. But, with Eva there with him, he felt his anger bubbling to the surface. The anger he felt when matters weren't in his control was now magnified by the factor of protective instinct.

No time to think... Or overthink.

Matthias's lunge at Balaclava was fast and violent, surprising himself and the assailant. A shove. A punch. Another punch. And another. Slamming Balaclava into the wall. The metallic clang and echo of the gun against the concrete floor. The attacker sliding from tile to floor. A kick. Two. Three. Four, five, six. Matthias was lashing out. The dull thud of boot against stomach bounced around the underpass.

Eva, her heart pounding, watched the violence unfold before her. Determination etched across Matt's face as he piled into the mugger. She felt sick. Scared. But not scared for her safety. That had been assured several kicks and punches ago. She was scared that Matt would go too far.

Summoning her own courage, she sprang into action. She knew that the escalation of violence could only lead to more dire consequences. With a surge of strength, she pulled Matt away from the assailant, her voice cutting through the chaos.

"Stop! Matt! Stop!... Stop!" Eva pleaded, her grip firm on Matt's shoulders.

Matthias, though wild with a mix of anger, fear and aggression, eased up when he felt Eva's touch and heard her voice, and slowed his attack on the man on the floor. Before, he would not have slowed down so quickly. But now...

"Matt, please!" Eva's voice, urgent and calming, penetrated the haze of the moment. "That's enough. He's had enough. It's okay... we're okay... I'm okay. I'm okay."

Matthias stopped. The underpass fell into an uneasy silence, with only his laboured breathing to be heard. His hair a floppy, sweaty mess, falling across his face. He could feel himself shaking. Eva held his face in her hands, calming him further.

Leaving the attacker curled up in the foetal position, Matthias ripped off the mugger's purple balaclava. He collected up the gun, put it in his jacket pocket, and felt it click against the lolly sticks.

"Matt, we said no guns -" Eva reminded him.

Matthias said nothing, simply handed her the purple balaclava.

Purple was Eva's favourite colour.

31:3

FOR SALE.

Renborough Brothers have the pleasure in offering to market this detached five-bedroom house with double-garage in a desirable and much sought after location. Nestled in the surrounding countryside, the property has ideal access to the local town of Renborough, with its mainline rail links and access to motorway networks. Once an old farmhouse, the property enjoys around six acres of wild and landscaped garden to the rear. The property is in need of modernisation...

"Modernisation is an understatement!" bellowed Jude in his familiar, overbearing manner. "Whole place needs new electrics, gas supply reconnection, new roof, new flooring. Fuckin' hell! Probably need the fuckin' chimney swept out and repointed. Bit beyond your skills, eh Matty! Luckily for you, I'll get Gez and Dizzy to do it," he declared, as he shoved the estate agent's house particulars back at Matthias, popped his glasses in his top pocket, and stomped out of the living room to explore the house further.

Matthias hated being called Matty. Jude knew this, of course, but didn't give a shit. He always called him Matty, which Matthias found very disrespectful, but doubted he'd ever earn any respect from Jude. The easiest thing for him to do was to smile and nod. He loved Jude's daughter, so he had to tolerate Jude, not like him. And Eva had reassured him last night and again this morning that she'd do what she could to control any strings her father put in front of them as a condition of him helping them buy the place.

Matthias absolutely trusted Eva.
Jude? Not so much.

* * * * *

Matthias and Eva had stumbled across the old farmhouse by accident last week.

They'd been out enjoying one of their usual meanders around the lakes, but at Eva's insistence that they 'follow their hearts and take a new path', they'd taken a more circuitous route home, through the surrounding countryside, out through the woods, and onward through green pastures and glorious golden rapeseed fields, back into fields framed by dry stone walls All of which they'd never visited before.

The warm, late afternoon summer sun on the day had made it a pleasant stroll. The walk through the unfamiliar environs had led them to the bottom of the property's acres of rear garden. Neither of them knew it was a garden - there was no fencing or clear boundary. It was only as they made their way through the wild and overgrown shrubs and bushes and grass and trees and reached the tired-looking, dirty pond, did they see the rear siding of the house, with its French doors and its wooden-framed windows still a couple of hundred feet away. Inviting and intriguing and haunting; drawing you nearer, teasing you to look inside.

They loved it. Rounding the plot and reaching the front of the house, they'd seen the FOR SALE sign, and had both fallen for the old building.

Finding this place felt like it was their destiny, their fate.

* * * * *

This morning, they'd agreed that they wouldn't tell Jude anything.

Eva had stated that she'd struggle with not saying anything because she'd neither hidden anything from, nor ever lied to, her father. They'd never lied to each other, she'd said adamantly. Matthias had gently coaxed her round and assured her that this wasn't lying, nor was it hiding things from him. Just for this first visit, they'd let Jude be Jude and deal with it together afterwards, avoid riling him up and arguing pointlessly with the man.

Let's just enjoy visiting the house.

As the two of them approached the property, Jude's old black pickup truck was already parked up, and he was standing next to the front door. His six-foot-five frame almost dwarfing the old farmhouse door, whose aging oak seemed to beckon you beyond the weathered exterior of the house, inviting you in to look around inside.

Seeing Jude standing there, and the old house perched ominously on the edge of the countryside, isolated from anywhere and everywhere, Matthias had some qualms and felt strangely anxious. He put it down to Jude's presence and the unknown of what lay behind the front door. Not a comforting combination.

But he shook it off.

Stepping in through the front door, the hallway foyer set itself at the corner of a right angle, heading off in two directions. To the right, the hallway headed past the living room and to the staircase; and straight ahead in the other direction, the hallway headed down past the dining room on the left and on into the kitchen.

The creaking floorboards whispered of years gone by as the three of them explored the decaying rooms. The old peeling wallpaper made the place look and feel cold and grey.

There was water for the taps and the toilets, which was encouraging, even if the old plumbing was noisy. And most of the rooms, where each old interior door had a lock-and-key, needed new furnishings and fixings and decorating. There was an old, solid, mahogany table in the dining room, an oval Formica table and four chairs in the kitchen, and a few old chairs and boxes in the basement, but not much else.

Yes, the whole place was a doer-upper, and most definitely in need of modernisation, but you could see its potential.

They were pleasantly surprised, as they stepped into the living room. There was a tired sofa, a leather wingback chair, and a gilt-framed Regency mirror above an ornate marble fireplace surround jutted up against the chimney stack in which nestled a rusting iron fire grate. But they reckoned they could make use of it all.

Eva wrapped her arms around Matthias and rested her head on his chest. He kissed the top of her head. Though he couldn't see her face, he could feel her smiling.

"I can see us snuggled up in front of an open fire at Christmas," Eva said, happily.

He placed an arm around her back and pulled her tighter. "I love this place, Eva. We'd make fantastic memories here. I can just see -"

Matthias didn't finish what he was saying, interrupted by Jude bellowing from the hallway, "That fuckin' basement is a cracker, Matty. It's all solid cold concrete and a solid wooden door. Fuckin' love it! I'll tell you what, the pair of ya, I'm gonna store wine down there. I'm gonna start collecting it. Retirement plans, yeah? Can't keep doing what I do forever, can I?" as he strode into the living room.

Eva squeezed Matthias tighter, keeping the conversation just between them. "I love it too. It needs colour, but we can do it.

We'll keep that leather chair, Matt. I love it. Love the shape…
the leather. It can be your chair. I can see you sitting there," Eva
said quietly, gazing up into Matthias' face. "And I'll just lounge
there on the sofa, like Lady Muck. We'll get it reupholstered -"

"I'll use this armchair when I visit," announced Jude,
flopping himself into the leather wingback, knowingly ruining
the moment again. "Suits me, this, eh, Evie?"

Matthias squeezed Eva, said he was going to take a further
look around the kitchen and the basement, and wandered off.

Matthias didn't like Jude.

Eva shuffled closer to the sofa, stared at her father. "Dad!
Stop winding Matt up, will you? Please." Eva dug at her father
when Matthias was out of earshot.

Jude, rising from the chair, "He's so bloody sensitive," he
sniped, moving to look out through the French doors, out into
the garden.

"He's struggling with the fact that we need your help to buy
this place. We'll pay you back. He's found a publisher for his
book. He's officially an author now -"

"You don't need to worry about that, Evie. You're my
daughter. I'm happy to help you. Haven't I always looked after
ya? You can't stay living in that pokey little hole you're in now, can
ya? My daughter deserves the best. Hey, my girl. Ain't that right?"

"We don't want any strings attached, Dad… we're worried
that you… it's just you helping us out, yeah?"

Jude remained quiet for a while, staring out of the French
doors. Eva flopped down onto the sofa and looked around the
room.

"Dad?"

"Your mum would've loved this place. Loved it. Don't you
think, Evie?" Jude said, knowing the effect the mention of her
mother would have on his daughter.

A pang of guilt rippled through Eva's chest and belly. She didn't want to acknowledge it. Deep-down she knew her father blamed her for her mother leaving. She didn't want to believe that, but she blamed herself, too.

Jude pulled a cigar from his top pocket, rolled it between his finger and thumb, popped it between his moistened lips, and lit it. "G and Diz, could probably tidy the garden up, too. Sort the electrics, the plumbing... even sort the basement. Good, solid blokes, they are," he stated through a puff of thick smoke.

"Please don't smoke, Dad."

"Shush! The fuck're you moaning about? It ain't gonna kill me." Jude turned and made his way to Eva. Cigar hanging from his mouth, he offered his hands to Eva. She reached her arms out to him in automatic reaction but stared at the floor. Jude held her hands in his, staring at them for a second or two too long, which made Eva look up at her father's face. As bullish as he could be, Jude knew this was not the time or place to say anything. He'd wait. He just pulled her up from the sofa. "Let's chat with Matty outside, shall we?"

As they'd suspected, Jude didn't make an offer of help. Jude laid out a deal. The deal. The deal was he'd give them the money they needed to buy the place, and they didn't need to pay him back unless they wanted to.

But the deal came with one condition.

A deal that Matthias knew was coming; was inevitable. It filled him with dread. He knew Eva would feel the entanglement of familial bonds battling the weight of the choice to be made. But if it meant he and Eva could live their own lives, their new lives, free of Jude's world, then it was a deal he... they could live with.

Destiny.

Fate.

Jude crushed and extinguished his cigar under foot, jumped up into his pickup. "I'm gonna love that basement... and that chair!" he shouted, not looking at them. He then pulled away with a spin of his truck's wheels, kicking up clumps of gravel.

Matt and Eva clambered into her little yellow car and followed a few moments later, watching the old farmhouse - now set to become their new home, their future - get smaller in the rear-view mirror.

* * * * *

Beside the tree, in the field opposite, on the other side of the hedged lane that led to and from the property, set against a bright yellow rapeseed field backdrop in the near distance, the grey-suited figure had watched their visit with interest, the shoots of a dark psychological dynamic unfolding.

There is an undeniable difference between destiny and fate: destiny is what you want, fate is what you get.

E | T

i speak with her

alone

then not alone

matt is there not

there   **purple**

denial

insanity inside of my head i am liminal

leave it for

dead

the house

i love you   two

we are liminal

sobbing tears

glass shattered splintered

tell me talk to me

time is not linear its irregular four

rheumy sclera   what is

going on outside of your mind

nina nonata

man comes home   he loves   woman please come

home   **she to edify me** six

coming home i am   **destiny fate** perdida

its hard to bear

i feel torment from deep within

i can't breathe   **cigarette**

pain   no

more

broken mirror   lolly sticks

winter venerable man

i need to breathe   **speak to the man**

saw you there always there

behind the locked

door of the big house   chimney   **handprint**

handprint handprint handprint **only when you feel so low**

do your feelings show   they are my dreams

i will dream them   now youre gone

crawl to the stars give your soul

and

deep in my heart   love is turmoil

eight

ink ink **ink**   **nine i need to hear you speak**

i wanted

ten everything with you **eidolon** can you hear me calling

bodach clink   **rasp**

fingers fingers **fingers**

youre everywhere except here   **clunk** see **she wants to**
meet me   closure **closure closure**

life love harmony

32:2

The morning at the lakes was a beautiful autumn one.

The birdsong was loud as Matt and Eva made their way through the woodland and meadow trails before reaching their favourite wooden bridge, spanning a small tributary that fed into (or was it from?) one of the mid-size lakes. It was a place they walked at least once, sometimes twice a week. Somewhere they could talk, hold hands, and get away from the small constricting space of their two-up, two-down terraced house in the crowded street in the poorer area of their grubby old part of town.

But they'd not have to put up with a lack of space for much longer.

Reluctant about accepting it, with some financial help from Jude, Eva's father, they could put in an offer on the old farmhouse. They knew Jude would put a condition on the money, but they'd agreed they could handle it. They were a team. And to share new lives together in their new, big house was worth one last 'Jude-ism', whatever it may be.

At the beginning of the conversations, Eva believed her father would be happy to give her the money. She was convinced he'd always looked after her, looked out for her. He'd brought her up on his own, made sacrifices, put food on the table, given her an education, and kept a roof over her head. He'd even signed up to satellite TV, so she could watch all her cartoons and teen-dramas when she was home for the holidays. Matt had felt like the bad guy to start with. He'd been polite, supporting and careful in his reminders to Eva that, based on conversations they'd had over the years - so words from her own mouth - her father had packed her off to boarding school when she was seven, stuck her in front of the TV during school holidays, and even employed a string of au pairs until she was old enough to be left alone. So, to Matt, he was convinced there'd be a quid pro quo.

And he'd convinced Eva to expect it.

But they both knew Jude was their only option.

They'd handle it.

Then they took the next step...

* * * * *

A call to Renborough Brothers Estate Agents to make an appointment to view the old farmhouse had gone well - no one else had enquired about it, so they could visit it whenever they wanted to. And when the agent had said the owner was happy to drop the price a little just for them, Matthias and Eva were walking on air, full of contentment.

* * * * *

Yes, the lakes were a beautiful place. Even more so now. It all felt like it was their place. Their world. Just for them.

The lakes were the third place they'd kissed. On their third date. Which was a few days after their cliché cinema/meal second date. Although Eva said that was their first official date, because it was a week after their first goodnight kiss on Eva's dad's doorstep, after Matthias had walked her home. Eva said that the first time they met didn't count as a date. Matthias disagreed. They were all dates.

It was the first place they'd made love. Under what had now become their favourite wooden bridge.

Matthias paused as they stepped onto the bridge and pulled Eva back by her left hand. She faced him. He squeezed her hand tightly and kissed her passionately. She responded in kind.

It definitely felt like it was their place.

Eva held Matt's hand and watched the stream flow beneath the bridge.

"You must miss your mum," Matt said quietly, his hand resting on hers as they leaned on the bridge's wooden rail.

A few seconds of thought and contemplation passed, then Eva said, "It was nice when Alma said she'd come through. I found it... comforting, you know?"

Matt said nothing.

"She said about the house, didn't she? My mum knew about the house, Matt. I've not said anything about the house to Alma. There's got to be something in it," Eva said, looking for some kind of confirmation.

Matt didn't believe in any of that spirit, medium malarkey, but he knew Eva did, and he knew she found comfort in it. More importantly, he knew Eva struggled with change and change was where their lives, their relationship, was at now. Not a crossroads, per se, but a fork in the road; a new direction to choose. And they were choosing it.

"You've got a lot on your mind, Evie, a lot of things going on... changing. Alma will know that."

"Don't belittle it, Matt, please. It's important to me." Eva pulled her hand away from beneath his.

"Sorry," Matthias looked out across the water. He was sorry that he'd not said the right thing. "It's just we have got changes happening... us, the house, your dad... And -"

Eva moved sideways, away from him. Just a foot or so. He could tell she was upset, and it stopped his attempted apologetic explanation from continuing.

"I'm just saying that Alma would've picked up on it. I'm not saying you told her…" he tried to add credence to what he was saying, but let his words fade off. *Not the right approach*, he decided.

The two of them stood silent for a few moments, both just leaning on the bridge rail, staring down at the rippling stream.

"I am sorry, gorgeous. I am," Matt spoke softly.

Eva continued to stare at the stream for a moment or two longer, before she responded. "I know, I know. You're right. I have got a lot on my mind. Us, our future. And. This house thing with my dad... it's... it's all just made me think of my mum. Dad was never the same when he lost her. I was there when she went, Matt... just stood there in the kitchen -"

"You were five, Eves -"

"Hollering, shouting, raised voices… I remember that… I heard the front door slam. I remember dad shouting and screaming after her. I remember him grabbing the breakfast items off the kitchen side and dropping the bowls and cups into the sink, chucking the Coco Pops into the cupboard. He put them in the wrong cupboard. Why do I remember that?"

Matt knew her mum had left when Eva was just five-years-old. And he knew her mum had died a couple of years later from cancer. But Eva had never spoken about it in this way before. And he'd never pushed her about it. He slid next to Eva and held her hand once more.

"I remember him saying that I shouldn't have my toys out in the kitchen at breakfast. They were on the kitchen side, he told me. I don't remember the toys. He grabbed them and stormed out of the kitchen. The front door slammed again. I don't really remember anything else until he came back and told me she was gone."

Matt squeezed her hand a little tighter.

"I didn't see her again until dad took me to the hospital to see her when she died. I remember her purple patched jacket and... I... I never got to speak to her, Matt," she choked back some tears. "After the funeral, he was so quiet... distant. I always felt it was my fault, somehow. Maybe my toys being all over the kitchen was too much? Maybe I was the reason she left? I just wanted my dad to be happy, to be okay," her voice quivered. "I struggle to shake the feeling, y'know? He wants to help me... us. He's offered us the money, Matt, and I can't not let him help... He's my dad -"

"And him helping us is okay, Eva. We just both know that it won't be an offer for us to consider. It'll be the money with strings attached."

"Maybe. Maybe a little tit for tat. Nothing we can't handle. I'll manage it. I'll talk to him, Matt... I promise," she forced a smile, attempting to give at least a small appearance of confidence.

Matthias said nothing. There was nothing he could say. Nothing he should say, he decided. He simply continued to hold Eva's hand as the two of them watched the water trickle and tumble under their bridge.

"Poohsticks?" Matthias eventually asked, as he pulled a collection of wooden lolly sticks from his jacket pocket. Eva loved an ice lolly during the summer, and he always saved the sticks solely for this tradition of theirs. He hoped it might be the diversion they needed.

Eva smiled, her mood lifting. She loved playing Poohsticks. She giggled and ran to the centre of the bridge, placed one hand on the ornate guardrail and danced a little dance. "Winner does a dare!", she shrieked.

"You're on." Matthias reached her and offered the sticks so she could choose the one she wanted.

The morning sun glistened off the stream's rippling flow as Matthias counted down from three. Eva dropped her stick on what was probably a count of two-point-eight - like she always did - but Matthias didn't care. He knew she was better at doing dares. Besides, he'd been daring enough dancing naked for her the other day. So, maybe she'd return the favour.

They watched their sticks pass under the bridge and took two quick strides across the narrow bridge to the other side, and leaned over the rail to watch the sticks emerge. Eva giggled and squealed with childish excitement, and Matthias really hoped the first stick through was hers.

33:1

Late afternoon, on the last day of what had been a fairly pleasant summer, the diminishing rays of the sun were streaking through the small bedroom-cum-office window. *Not enough room to swing a cat*, Matthias thought, let alone accommodate a desk and his laptop, on which he was tapping away. A cigarette burning in the ashtray next to his silver cigarette case.

He was not quite finding his usual solace and comfort he got from writing and smoking. Writing and smoking were things he could control and, most of the time, they usually quieted his mind; he found they gave him some respite from his overthinking.

But not today. Today he was overthinking plenty.

Spinning his Zippo between finger and thumb, clicking its lid open and clunking it closed, his mind was bouncing thoughts around his head like a jumbled mess of puzzle pieces strewn around his grey matter. Not pieces from a single jigsaw, but shapes and colours and patterns from a myriad of jigsaws. No order to any of it. Just... just a hodgepodge.

Thinking that he needed to get some cigarettes; he only had three left. Thinking about what he'd like to buy when his upfront payment came in from his publisher. Thinking about whether the public would like his book. Thinking about the story he was currently writing. Thinking about what he had to do, to learn, to understand, to be careful of and knowledgeable about, now he was in the world of being a published author. Thinking about some lyrics for the tunes in his head.

Thinking about life - his journey in it; his dreams, his future, his destiny, his fate.

Thinking about lolly sticks.

Thinking about this little terraced house he and Eva were renting. Money down the drain, month-after-month-after-month.

Built in the early part of the twentieth century, the architect and the builders had no foresight nor consideration for the lifestyles and needs of future generations; they had not designed rooms to accommodate large televisions, big sofas, king-size beds (let alone queen-size), wardrobes, showers, fridge-freezers. Not a desk. Not even a laptop. You name it; it didn't fit into this small square footage.

Nor had history's construction industry applied any forethought to the future of the motor car. There was no space for on- or off-street parking outside their house, not even for Eva's little yellow Fiat. They'd often have to park a street or two away, and the car was tiny, for goodness' sake.

Yep. Thinking about somewhere bigger and better to live, something that would be theirs. His and Eva's.

Thinking about cigarettes, words, lyrics, tunes, cars.

Cars. A car.

Pretty much at the top of his shopping list, with money from his new publisher. Okay, so the buses around Renborough were fairly frequent, and the onward public transport connections pretty good, but he wanted the freedom and ability to travel when and where he desired and needed to go. Hoping that now his writing career was taking a foothold, there'd be a much greater need for him to get out-and-about to find inspiration, research new locations, and invent stories, write words and lyrics and poetry.

Driving his new car to wonderful places faded from his mind, and the small room closed in on him, and he thought about their need for more space once again.

Thinking about the visit to the property they were viewing later this week. The house that Eva had fallen in love with. Which meant that Matthias had fallen in love with it, too. Which meant they'd need some extra money to buy it. Which meant that their only way to get the money they needed to buy the house and pursue their destiny, their fate, was through Eva's father, Jude. And Jude was a *narcissistic cunt*, as far as Matt was concerned; he disliked him. He knew they'd end up being beholden to him; Jude wouldn't give money out without some tit for tat.

Matt found it hard to believe that a father would put conditions on lending his own daughter some money, particularly as Jude had money. But, then again, he didn't put Jude in any kind of 'father-figure role-model' category. *Oh well, we'll see.*

Yep, all that was rolling around in his mind. And it was all made worse because Jude had insisted on visiting the property with them.

Christ! Thoughts. Thinking. Think, think, think, think, think!

Thinking of asking Eva to marry him.

Today.

Now.

He already had the ring in his desk drawer. He'd bought it over the phone directly from the jeweller as soon as they'd got home from their last weekend trip away. He loved trips away with Eva. She'd laugh her cackly laugh and say that she was brilliant on holidays. And he'd agree. She was definitely a five-star rating on Tripadvisor, he'd say to her. She loved to look in all the little shops and jewellers. Never wanting to buy anything, just steal it. He didn't like that side of her - she got it from her father.

Clicking and twirling his silver Zippo between thumb and forefinger, taking a drag on his cigarette, he remembered how her face lit up when she saw the ring in the shop window, and he'd listened to the comment she made.

Now to pluck up the courage to ask her. And work out how to ask her.

Think, man.

Think.

* * * * *

Eva was in their small living room at the front of the house, lounging on the sofa, and despite it being a warm pleasant summer afternoon, she was cuddling beneath her purple comfort blanket, finishing her ice lolly, flicking through her phone, whiling away time for no particular reason - because that's what people do, she figured.

Though, deep-down, she knew it was a way of deflecting her own anxiety.

She didn't like change.

She'd recently been thinking about how life might change, might need to change... will need to change. Matt was now a published author. And a move to a new house. And... well, it wasn't a new house, as such. It was an old farmhouse.

Anyway, change was coming.

After she'd returned home from her last robbery, she and Matt had spoken seriously about the future. She knew he didn't like what she did; didn't like that part of her. He absolutely adored everything else about her - her shoulder length autumnal balayage hair, her blue eyes, her soft lips, her nose that got all scrunched up when she was trying to concentrate or read, her cackling laugh, the way she pushed her reading glasses back up her nose when they slipped a little, leaving fingerprints all over lenses. Not a good practice for a petty criminal, Matt would say.

She often saw him staring at her, smiling. He'd demand a kiss pretty much each-and-every time he saw her, even if she simply left the room and then returned. He'd leave her little love notes and poems. She loved those. She always took a photo of them with her phone and kept the notes in her bedside drawer. A fly-on-the-wall might say he was weak and needy and lacking self-esteem. Emasculated, perhaps. But she knew he had a powerful and strong side, even an anger at times. Rare times, but it could be there.

Yes, sometimes she felt overwhelmed with his affection, but not suffocated.

She didn't doubt his love.

And she loved him.

Loved his handsome looks, his floppy dirty-blond mop of hair, his gorgeous nose. Adored his creativity. Loved watching him write.

But she knew something was on his mind.

Something was on her mind, too. But she'd deflect it for now and think about Matt and what was bugging him.

She was sure it wasn't the silver Zippo lighter she'd got for him. Yes, it had come from her last robbery, but she'd got it engraved with a small heart and the letters M&E before she'd given it to him. On reflection, she thought it looked a bit tacky, but Matt said he really liked it. Loved it, in fact. He said he loved the sound it made when he opened and closed it, loved the feel of the rasp and roll of the flint wheel. No, it wasn't the Zippo on his mind. It wasn't the robberies she did; he always knew that about her. Besides, she was doing fewer now than she'd ever done, making a conscious and concerted effort to over the last couple of years they'd been together.

It wasn't the general talk of their future they'd had. They both wanted to be together forever. That was their destiny. But maybe it was about a particular part of their conversation about the future.

She knew it was about the role her father would play in it. She would need to manage her father's overbearing manner, need to manage her own feelings of guilt she associated with him. Feelings that were now coming more to the surface. And all the while, supporting her's and Matt's desire that this was to be their future. *A future without paternal strings attached,* she wondered.

She was fairly confident that it'd be okay.

Fairly.

She pulled her blanket a little tighter, clicked onto social media and dropped a message to her spiritualist. A visit to her for an insight into the future would definitely help ease her anxiety.

* * * * *

Hips gyrating and penis swinging, Matthias danced naked into the front room, singing one of his own songs. Giving his movement a ballroom step and glide from doorway to sofa, "I wanted to dance with you," he sang the melody, his vocal a smooth, soulful timbre to compliment the style of the song they both knew.

What a sight! Eva cackled with laughter, and chimed in with, "I just knew it was right." She knew the song. She made Matt sing it to her from time to time.

"A desire for you," Matt sang the next line, dancing steps toward the sofa.

"From that very first night," she laughed as she sang.

"Oh-oh-ohhhh," they wailed in unison.

He danced along the length of the sofa, warbling the next line, "We danced beneath the stars," and jiggling his genitals as he went, continuing with, "And I heard angels crying -"

"A kiss and a promise," they sang together.

"Before we said goodbye," This was the line that was worrying him, seeing as what he had planned kind of contradicted both the lyrics and his feelings. He would never say goodbye to Eva, couldn't imagine his life without her. But he had to keep the moment going, keep the song going, he thought, as he loomed over Eva and leant his head down to kiss her.

"I miss you," she sang the line, "and I miss your love," she managed to warble before Matt planted a kiss on her. She liked it when he was above her.

"I love you, just because," they sang together, before the two of them laughed loudly and finished their kiss.

Not the greatest piece of writing he'd done; bit cheesy was Matt's opinion of his own composition. It was a song he'd written for Eva when they were first dating. It was more of a pop music track, digressing from his more favoured darker rock and punk tastes. But it was a very personal song written for Eva, so he loved to sing it for her, with her. Driven by the early desires and lust and infatuation and blindness that comes with a new and blossoming love relationship, and with Eva's encouragement, he'd recorded the song and submitted it into the Eurovision Song Contest entry competition. He'd never heard anything back. No real surprise to him.

"I love you, Eva." Matt whispered. His lips hover above hers, his eyes engaged with hers. "I love kissing you."

"Maybe we should get married?" she smiled.

Matthias smiled, "I do."

"Oh, you do, do you?" she chuckled.

"Until death do us part," he added. And he meant it.

"And even after that?" Eva smirked, tilted her head and raised an eyebrow, questioning.

"Even after that," he assured her.

She lightly dragged her nails down his back, and let her eyes travel downward, taking in his chin, his chest, his stomach, his...

"Come upstairs," Matt says, standing back up, taking her hand in his.

Off they skipped. Matthias led Eva by the hand. Eva cackling with laughter, watching his hairless buttocks bounce as they ascend the thirteen steps of the narrow stairs, treading the carpet whose pattern would suit any Wetherspoons.

As they approached the master bedroom, Matt darted behind Eva and placed his hands over her eyes. "No peeking," he whispered in her ear, and shuffled her into the bedroom, stopping at the foot of the bed. "Open your eyes," he said, removing his hands.

There, on the wall, above the bed's headboard, are eight multicoloured Post-its:

MARRY ME?

Eva stood stock still for a moment, simply staring at the words. Tears of joy filled her eyes. She turned to smile and talk to Matt, but he's not there. She swivels her head, her eyes, to look around the room to find him. Then, returning to the doorway of the bedroom, Matt's there, dropped onto one knee, holding an open ring box.

"Marry me?" he asked.

"Really!?" Eva asked, sounding surprised, her breath taken away. "Why?" she giggled.

"Just because."

Struggling to get the words out through the lump in her throat, and struggling to see the ring or Matt clearly, her watery eyes blurring the scene before her, she simply smiled the biggest smile he'd ever witnessed, her face lighting up.

She nodded, "I will."

* * * * *

The light outside was fading. Matthias drew the curtains, then slumped back into the corner of the sofa, and Eva snuggled into him, pulling her purple blanket over her. To her, the ring sparkled, even in the low front room lamplight. It would've sparkled in complete darkness, as far as she was concerned. She couldn't be happier.

But now the thing she'd deflected earlier was now creeping to the forefront of her mind.

"Are you happy?" she asked him, as she looked up into his blue eyes.

He smiled, "Too right, I am. I've just asked the most gorgeous girl in the world to be my wife and she said yes. I'm the happiest man alive. I can even face your dad. The future starts today, yeah?"

Eva smiled, but an anxious one. "Matt, I've something I need to tell you," she said, pulling and scruffing her blanket into a ball and holding it to her chest and belly.

He pulled her in tight; to give her the reassurance and security he felt she needed so she could speak her mind.

"I've made another appointment to see Alma. Get some advice. Get a steer on the future. Keep picking the right path, y'know? I've been having some weird dreams... of my parents... when I was a child... Alma says my mother came through... she's happy... she's pleased that I... says my future involves a new house. I'm in a liminal state, apparently."

Matt said nothing.

"Before you start, I know you don't like Alma, but she gives me a lot of comfort. I like her. I trust her. I've made an appointment to see her again... for another reading." Eva continued.

Normally, Matthias might've gone into a sulk or a strop, but not today. He was far too happy to react in his usual negative, derogatory manner with the subject of Alma. "If it helps you, babes, that's good enough for me. Is that what you wanted to tell me?"

Eva shook her head, pulled her blanket bundle a little tighter into a fluffy purple ball, holding it a little closer to her belly.

Looking up Matt's beautiful blue eyes, Eva whispered...

34:0

"I'm pregnant."

más allá de lo natural

Yes, she was pregnant.

That wasn't clear to me during our sessions.

In my line of work, it can take me some time to decipher the messaging and voices, visions and feelings my gift gives me. By the time I had understood, it was too late, she had already committed to taking the path. I'm not saying things would have turned out any different, that's not how this works, but maybe it could have been... I don't know... more peaceful?

Maybe a thinner piece of ink, en memoria? Half-a-ring around my pinkie, perhaps?

I'm normally apathetic to my clients – though I do put on the necessary act to convince them and reel them in - but there was something unusual about her.

I really liked her.

She had been to see me a few times over the summer and into the early autumn and I liked her from the first meeting. We had a rapport. There was something unusual, something different about her. She had an unusual way of life, didn't have a mundane day-to-day job. The way she looked; she was incredibly cute and beautiful. She loved and was loved deeply. Things she said. Things she didn't say. The distorted view of her relationship with her father, and why and how she lost her mother. None of it particularly unusual or puzzling, but she was definitely different...

She had the 'gift'.

It was buried deep inside her. She wasn't aware of it. I thought I recognised the signs early on, but they were weak, hidden. It wasn't until after all the loss, when we met again, did we both become sure of her gift and embrace it. I found it somewhat overwhelming and exhilarating. I like to think she did too.

Maybe that was why I liked Eva.

Más allá de lo natural... Beyond natural.

What follows is an annotation of pages of notes and scribbles, taken during her visits...

Alma Sofia

|E

i speak with her i need to see her forked road anxiety give me a
path to walk I never saw her we never spoke take the path
summer for sale woman is gone matt is there dancing naked
penis writing for me the stone sparkles toys cluttered alone then
not alone the woman with the beautiful face toys on the kitchen
worktop new toy is cold heavy shiny matt is there not there
shades of purple woman shouts man shouts no love but then
love but then nurturing nurturing nurturing lies hands up in
summer embarazada denial shook three cigarettes his head in
indignation mauve and violet door slams man tell me of the
woman flailing her arms hitting the man autumn hitting the
man hitting the man not the child lies he lied finger on the steel
pistol weighted heavy in the cupboard wrong cupboard sale
agreed take me to the edge steal steal steal my daily bread
insanity inside of my head i am liminal black is white all i see is
red silver silver silver glints and sparkles child heartbeat
heartbeat heartbeat hearbeat crossroads pick a path pick up the
toy colours pictures echoes steal it use it abuse it leave it for
dead the lakes shouting matt is there on his knee recoil from the
backlash of what you said the bridge the house sanctuary
grabbing the toys i love you he smells of coffee two the heavy
toy the front door slams weightless no lies no secrets yellow car
the child standing still sobbing silent silence we are liminal
birdsong just because quiet sobbing tears money eyes stinging
glass shattered splintered matt is rambunctious dirty sweaty
watching writing and singing and humming then i start to feel

alone tell me talk to me guide arms hold me me minutes pass hour hours pass time is not linear its irregular four in space in time rheumy sclera dust metal sulphur fire what is going on outside of your mind what are you hiding from i am floating nina nonata what are you looking for narcissist man comes home charred he loves me woman please come home he does not love me she to edify me six shrieking at the men murmuration of starlings i know the woman is not coming home i am coming home destiny fate perdida on the red bus the land is not green and fair its hard to bear and i feel and i feel torment from deep within razor cuts blood and diamond ring footsteps footsteps footsteps beneath the skin decaying rooms child stay down on the ground all around theres no sound just watching you bleed grievous i just knew your face man in the glasses holds the child heartbeat heartbeat heartbeat the child feels him squeeze her shoulders i can't breathe kiss her hair the toy two cigarettes is gone not to be talked about no more shouting bodily heat pain joy no more bad words television ten thousand stations switch in on mesmerise the girl cold egomaniacal egomaniacal egomaniacal concrete broken mirror broken sticks lolly sticks and stones no words spoken in the home harm winter venerable man nina nonato not venerable outside lost found love is thrown i need to breathe flicker flame scented speak to the man nothing feels fine money i saw you there always there your face remembered locked in my mind matthias writing creating for me in the back seat of a black car behind the locked door of the big house sold chimney smoke handprint handprint handprint handprint only when you feel so low do your feelings show words melodies they are my dreams i will dream them scream of swifts now youre gone bleed scream crawl to the stars give your soul so crawl phone ringing and pinging and and remember better days negotiate not offer deep in my heart tobacco love is turmoil the soil the voices in my head tears it apart eight distant muffled colours rainbow ink ink ink the taste nine i need to hear you speak deep in my heart youve been away for so long i wanted nothing from you ten everything with you eidolon can you hear me calling bodach clink you never reply you gave me life rasp she was like water through my fingers fingers fingers like the breeze youre everywhere except here you clunk see she wants to meet me wants to look me in the eye closure closure closure life love harmony born a million lies

NOW

Early autumn.

FOR SALE.

Renborough Brothers have the pleasure of offering to market this detached five-bedroom house with double-garage in a desirable and sought after location. Nestled in the surrounding countryside, the property has ideal access to the local town of Renborough, with its mainline rail links and access to motorway networks. Once an old farmhouse, the property enjoys around six acres of wild and landscaped garden to the rear. The property is in need of modernisation...

She stopped reading at that point and placed the estate agent's house particulars onto the kitchen table next to her laptop and the burning scented candle. She chuckled to herself about the property needing modernisation. *It need quite more than*, she thought.

But she was satisfied with the asking price, it would draw people in - *vuela a la mierda*, like flies to a spider's web.

She admired the estate agent's enthusiasm and courage in keeping the property on their books. They'd had it listed on-and-off for several years but, despite keen expressions of interest, potential buyers seemed to drop into radio silence. So, it hadn't sold. Of course, the agent had often asked her why she wanted to sell and why she didn't just live here. She always gave the same response - stony silence. But burning inside of her was the mantra she'd held for a long time - if this could not be her forever home, couldn't be the home she could live in and share with *her lover*, then she'd make it a forever home for other young lovers. A home for eternity.

She was thankful that Renborough Brothers' recent visit to measure up again and take some newer photos had been brief. No questions this time. And she admired herself for cleaning the place up. She'd carefully guided the estate agent around the property, of course. And they were polite enough to not mention the dustcovers and the undercurrent of lingering odours.

The needle scratched and stung and itched and pinched as she pushed it into her left ring finger's intermediate phalange, inking an eleventh stripe between the proximal and distal joints. This was her first premature tattoo (she'd not yet decided on the in memoriam one); she usually waited until... after. *But what harm could there be in prediciendo el future?* Besides, she was finding the pain addictive and quite pleasurable. Yes, it made her wince, brought tears to her eyes, but it meant everything to her. What had started as a way of punishing herself - sticking herself with needles and pins - had long been surpassed with thoughts of *his tattoos*, which she loved, and which led her to use the chastisement to remember *him*. The suffering she'd been through... was still going through. The not knowing. Not being able to contact *him*, to even speak to *him*. To find *him*.

* * * * *

They'd been so happy and in love and were talking about getting married, starting a family. That was when the two of them had found this house, all those winters ago. Their offer had been accepted and they'd moved in the day before Christmas Eve.

On the days leading up to the final moving-in day, she'd been away at a retreat, and he'd spent several days clearing the house, moving in some old second-hand furniture, fixing old floorboards, replacing a few broken windowpanes, getting the chimney swept and cleared. It had been a frantic time and they'd not had a spare moment to get any decorations or gifts.

As evening darkness drew in on that Christmas Eve, the two of them were snuggled up on the old sofa, settled and happy - she wrapped in his thick, tattooed arms in front of the old fireplace, the flames from the burning packing boxes making it as cosy as it could be.

Watching the flames flicker and dance, they'd sat for an hour or so in content silence.

Or so she'd thought.

"I can't do this anymore. I'm sorry," he'd said.

She had dreamed of wonderful Christmas, but that had now been taken from her. Happiness gone. Forever... gone. No gifts, no lover, no spirit and magic of Christmas. No Santa Claus.

After he had gone, she watched the fire die away to embers and ash.

She remained staring into the blackened fireplace all through Christmas Day and Boxing Day...

It was the longest of winters.

He never returned.

* * * * *

If she couldn't live here with *her lover*, then...

Finishing the new black stripe and dabbing the blood spots with her white silk pocket square, she then extinguished the candle's flame between the thumb and forefinger, snuffing it out with a pfft. She stared out through the window, running her long white fingernails through her long jet-black hair, caressing her rosary in her newly inked hand. Staring through the window's condensation at the dawn breaking over the garden, she thought it was bigger than six acres. But what did she know? She wasn't an estate agent.

Her laptop pinged to remind her of a session booked for later this morning with 'Becky' of Rebecca and Greg. Another young couple seeking advice. No doubt full of hopes and dreams, of destiny and fate, questions and guidance, like they all are. A young couple in need of her puppetry in motion. *Marionetas en movimiento*, she thought.

This return visit to the old farmhouse had been one with a particular purpose. She needed to collect the one item she desired but had stupidly forgotten the last time or two she was here. Luckily, the estate agent hadn't wanted to view the garden, which was where she needed to go now. Besides, the early morning air seemed like a pleasant way to finish the morning.

There was a morning chill in the air, so she'd forgone her usual suit and waistcoat attire and had popped her grey jacket over one of *his* old, black hooded sweatshirts. She pulled up the hood and made her way out of the kitchen, through the hallway, into the living room - its furniture mostly hidden under sack-cloth dust sheets. She glanced at the discoloured patch above the ornate marble mantelpiece and shook her head in puzzlement at the returning greasy handprint on the chimney breast where the grand Regency mirror had been. It hadn't been there when the estate agent was here, she was sure of that. She'd tried to clean it up during her previous visits, but there it was, a stubborn stain, a reminder. A further visitation to try to get it shifted, she thought. Permanently. With a shake of her head and a deep inhale of breath, she stepped out through the French doors that led to the garden.

She'd not been in the garden for a long time. Lying beneath this morning's early autumn mist, if felt somewhat foreboding. It looked very much unattended, unlikely it had seen any of kind of gardener for months – actually, it was unlikely it had seen anyone green-fingered since the sale before the one before last. *Six tattooed rings ago?* she wondered, - as the long, wet grass dampened her bare feet and reached halfway up her shins, painting them with the early morning frosty dew.

Nestled in and around the acres of land, landscaped with bushes and hedges and some fruit trees, and set off by the ornamental pond offset between bushes over on the west boundary of the garden, the garden was at odds with itself – the ability to create disquietude and anxiety, whilst being altogether a tranquil setting.

Had Eva and Matthias taken in this messy, overgrown, yet wonderful garden when they'd first viewed the house? She thought it was likely only when they first found the house, particularly if they'd taken an alternative path home from the lakes.

And with that thought in her head, she smiled beneath her black hood, and strode toward a landscaped plot of thick evergreen bushes. There the shovel stood erect, held in the ground by its blade. And draped over its handle the purple blanket, cold and damp. Not surprising, seeing as how long it had been here, exposed to the weather.

She noticed that the mist hadn't settled here.

What thoughts had been going around in his head? It must've been spinning like crazy. What feelings, emotions were coursing through him, as he'd dug into the autumn soil? Soil hard enough to present some resistance at the surface, but damper and softer below, once the sharp blade of the heavy shovel had broken through the first few inches of frosted earth.

Did he think it was his only option? Was it his first thought? Had he considered any other course of action as he sat in the leather armchair? Apparently not.

Lifting the blanket and wandering back toward the house, she paused at the bottom edge of the pond. She noticed that the low-hanging mist wasn't settling here, either. She always believed that mist over water was more likely, especially if it was everywhere else. But it was like the mist refused to hover above the pond. It was only a second's thought because she also noticed a black and silver shape beneath the pond's surface. Somehow, the early morning dawn sun was reflecting off the object. She didn't know that could happen. *Was reflecting the right word?* The word *refraction* sprang to her mind. She knew the pond was fairly shallow - probably only a couple of feet deep - so she guessed the sunlight, weak as it was at this time of day, could reach beneath the surface and put a little spotlight on what may lie below.

Had he stopped in this exact spot? Was she standing where he had stood? Where he'd made another decision? The decision to dispose of the gun, drop it into the pond? She didn't know. She should've asked him, of course, but the setting and the time hadn't been right at their last meeting.

She wouldn't retrieve the gun from the pond. Whilst the gun itself would be a useful object, she would have to make do with the purple blanket. Besides, she'd get wet, and it was too cold to be wet. Damp feet were fine. Her cropped trousers, finishing just below the knee, might avoid the water, but they might not. Wet legs, and potentially wet trousers would be uncomfortable. Not to mention traipsing water through the house. Or being damp and cold until she returned to her workplace for her session with Rebecca. *"Please, call me Becky. I prefer it," she'd said.*

No, the blanket would suffice. It's what she had come back for. She'd fold it neatly and place it on her shelf of knick-knacks.

She headed toward the house, back through the living room, out into the hallway, out the front door, passing the FOR SALE sign.

And, as she walked down the quiet, frosted lane, away from the property, she wrapped the purple blanket around her shoulders and began planning the upcoming session with Becky.

AGAIN

"Hola, soy Alma. Gracias por llamar. Por favor, deja tu nombre, tu número y un breve mensaje, y me pondré en contacto contigo tan pronto como sea posible. Gracias."

"Alma, it's Greg. I'm looking for Becky…"

ACKNOWLEDGEMENTS

My thanks go to my wife and my children for their support and love. Thank you, of course, to my parents, Menna and Derek. And my thanks to Tim and Warren, good friends who believed in this story way back in 2011 and helped to draft the script and shoot the film. The story has changed a bit since then, fellas, so I hope you enjoy it.

Finally, a thank you to you, the reader, for taking a couple of hours to read this story. I hope you enjoy it, too.

Front cover by Ashleigh Pollard

ABOUT THE AUTHOR

Solomon Oliver Black is a pseudonym.

But you guessed that, didn't you?

The name came about from two songs – *'Oliver'*, written by the real me back in the early 1990s, and *'Black'* by Pearl Jam (one of my favourite songs).

Yep. You guessed it again. The real me is a failed 'wannabe' rock star.

After spending most of the 1990s and early 2000s trying and practicing and recording (rinse-and-repeat), it never happened. Life and love and children and a dog have kept me happily distracted and busy and given me new dreams, new purpose… and still do. Though I have added a Harley Davidson to the list, so that's one teenage dream ticked off.

But I've now reached an age where I want to try again to fill the creative hole that still looms inside me, so I wrote this novella. If I can't be a rockstar, maybe I can be a writer?

Asrevni Inversa started life back in 2011 as a film script under a different name. A couple of friends and I did shoot the film over five days and nights… but it's best left locked away gathering dust, trust me.

So, Solomon wasn't born in Wokingham, Berkshire back in the summer of '69 (no, I'm not him) and he hasn't lived in Woodley, Reading for most of his 55 years.

But I was and I have.

SolomonOliverBlack.com

Summer 2024.